Paul's blue-eyed gaze bore into me. There wasn't the slightest hint of a smile on his face anymore. "Suze, when are you going to get it?"

That was when I finally noticed how close his face was to mine. Just inches away, really. I started instinctively to pull away, but the fingers that had been holding down Dr. Slaski's papers suddenly lifted and seized my wrist. I looked down at Paul's hand. His tanned skin was very dark against mine.

"Jesse's dead," Paul said. "But that doesn't mean you have to act like you are, too."

"I don't," I protested. "I—"

But I didn't get to finish my little speech, because right in the middle of it, Paul leaned over and kissed me.

Books by Meg Cabot

THE MEDIATOR 1: SHADOWLAND
THE MEDIATOR 2: NINTH KEY
THE MEDIATOR 3: REUNION
THE MEDIATOR 4: DARKEST HOUR
THE MEDIATOR 5: HAUNTED
THE MEDIATOR 6: TWILIGHT

THE PRINCESS DIARIES
THE PRINCESS DIARIES, VOLUME II: PRINCESS IN THE SPOTLIGHT
THE PRINCESS DIARIES, VOLUME III: PRINCESS IN LOVE
THE PRINCESS DIARIES, VOLUME IV: PRINCESS IN WAITING
THE PRINCESS DIARIES, VOLUME IV AND A HALF: PROJECT PRINCESS
THE PRINCESS DIARIES, VOLUME V: PRINCESS IN PINK
THE PRINCESS DIARIES, VOLUME VI: PRINCESS IN TRAINING
THE PRINCESS PRESENT: A PRINCESS DIARIES BOOK
PRINCESS LESSONS: A PRINCESS DIARIES BOOK
PERFECT PRINCESS: A PRINCESS DIARIES BOOK

ALL-AMERICAN GIRL
TEEN IDOL
NICOLA AND THE VISCOUNT
VICTORIA AND THE ROGUE
THE BOY NEXT DOOR
BOY MEETS GIRL
EVERY BOY'S GOT ONE

THE 1-800-WHERE-R-YOU BOOKS:
WHEN LIGHTNING STRIKES
CODE NAME CASSANDRA
SAFE HOUSE
SANCTUARY

MEG CABOT

the mediator
Haunted

avon books
AN IMPRINT OF HARPERCOLLINS PUBLISHERS

Library of Congress Catalog Card Number: 2004093416
ISBN 0-06-075164-9
First Avon edition, 2005

AVON TRADEMARK REG. U.S. PAT. OFF. AND IN OTHER COUNTRIES,
MARCA REGISTRADA, HECHO EN U.S.A.

❖

Visit us on the World Wide Web!
www.megcabot.com
www.harperteen.com
11 12 13 OPM 20 19 18 17 16 15 14 13 12

For Benjamin

Many thanks to Jennifer Brown,
Laura Langlie, Abigail McAden, and
Ingrid van der Leeden.

Fog. That's all I can see. Just fog, the kind that pours in from the bay every morning, seeping over my bedroom windowsills and spilling onto the floor in cold, ropy tendrils. . . .

Only here there are no windows, or even a floor. I am in a corridor lined with doors. There is no ceiling overhead, just coldly winking stars in an inky black sky. The long hall made up of closed doors seems to stretch out forever in all directions.

And now I'm running. I'm running down the corridor, the fog seeming to cling to my legs as I go, the closed doors on either side of me a blur. There's no point, I know, in opening any of these doors. There's nothing behind them that can help me. I've got to get out of this hallway, only I can't, because it just keeps getting longer and longer, stretching out into the darkness, still blanketed in that thick white fog. . . .

And then suddenly, I'm not alone in that fog. Jesse is there with me, holding my hand. I don't know if it's the warmth of his fingers or the kindness of his smile that banishes my fear, but suddenly, I am convinced that everything is going to be all right.

At least until it becomes clear that Jesse doesn't know the way out any more than I do. And now even the fact that my hand is in his can't squelch the feeling of panic bubbling up inside of me.

But wait. Someone is coming toward us, a tall figure striding through the fog. My frantically beating heart—the only sound I can hear in this dead place, with the exception of my own breathing— slows somewhat. Help. Help at last.

Except that when the fog parts and I recognize the face of the person ahead of us, my heart starts pounding more loudly than ever. Because I know he won't help us. I know he won't do a thing.

Except laugh.

And then I'm alone again, only this time, the floor beneath me has dropped away. The doors disappear, and I am teetering on the brink of a chasm so deep, I cannot see the ground below. The fog swirls around me, spilling into the chasm and seeming intent on taking me with it. I am waving my arms to keep from falling, grabbing frantically for something, anything, to hold on to.

Only there's nothing to grab. A second later, an unseen hand gives a single push.

And I fall.

chapter one

"Well, well, well," said a distinctly masculine voice from behind me. "If it isn't Susannah Simon."

Look, I won't lie to you. When a cute guy talks to me—and you could tell from this guy's voice that he was easy on the eyes; it was in the self-confidence of those *well, well, well*s, the caressing way he said my name—I pay attention. I can't help it. I'm a sixteen-year-old girl, after all. My life can't revolve entirely around Lilly Pulitzer's latest tankini print and whatever new innovations Bobbi Brown has made in the world of stay-put lip liner.

So I'll admit that, even though I have a boyfriend—even if *boyfriend* is a little optimistic a term for him—as I turned around to see the hottie who was addressing me, I gave my hair a little bit of a toss. Why shouldn't I? I mean, considering all the product I'd layered into it that morning, in honor of the first day of my junior year—not to mention the marine fog that regularly turns my head into a frizzy mess—my coiffure was looking exceptionally fine.

It wasn't until I'd given the old chestnut mane a flip that I turned around and saw that the cutie who'd said my name was not someone I'm too fond of.

In fact, you might say I have reason to be scared to death of him.

I guess he could read the fear in my eyes—carefully done up that morning with a brand-new combination of eye shadows called Mocha Mist—because the grin that broke out across his good-looking face was slightly crooked at one end.

"Suze," he said in a chiding tone. Even the fog couldn't dull the glossy highlights in his raffishly curly dark hair. His teeth were dazzlingly white against his tennis tan. "Here I am, nervous about being the new kid at school, and you don't even have a hello for me? What kind of way is that to treat an old pal?"

I continued to stare at him, perfectly incapable

of speech. You can't talk, of course, when your mouth has gone as dry as . . . well, as the adobe brick building we were standing in front of.

What was he doing here? *What was he doing here?*

The thing of it was, I couldn't follow my first impulse and run screaming from him. People tend to talk when they see impeccably garbed girls such as me run screaming from seventeen-year-old studlies. I had managed to keep my unusual talent from my classmates for this long, I wasn't about to blow it now, even if I was—and believe me, I *was*—scared to death.

But if I couldn't run away screaming, I could certainly move huffily past him without a word, hoping he would not recognize the huffiness for what it really was—sheer terror.

I don't know whether or not he sensed my fear. But he sure didn't like my pulling a prima donna on him. His hand flew out as I attempted to sweep past him, and the next thing I knew, his fingers were wrapped around my upper arm in a viselike grip.

I could, of course, have hauled off and slugged him. I hadn't been named Girl Most Likely to Dismember Someone back at my old school in Brooklyn for nothing, you know.

But I'd wanted to start this year off right—in Mocha Mist and my new black Club Monaco capris (coupled with a pink silk sweater set I'd snagged for a song at the Benetton outlet up in Pacific Grove)—not in a fight. And what would my friends and schoolmates think—and, since they were milling all around us, tossing off the occasional "Hi, Suze," and complimenting me on my ever-so-spiffy ensemble, they were bound to notice—if I began freakishly to pummel the new guy?

And then there was the unavoidable fact that I was pretty convinced that, if I took a whack at him, he might try to whack me back.

Somehow I managed to find my voice. I only hoped he didn't notice how much it was shaking. "Let go of my arm," I said.

"Suze," he said. He was still smiling, but now he looked and sounded slyly knowing. "What's the matter? You don't look very happy to see me."

"Still not letting go of my arm," I reminded him. I could feel the chill from his fingers—he seemed to be completely cold-blooded in addition to being preternaturally strong—through my silk sleeve.

He dropped his hand.

"Look," he said, "I really am sorry. About the

way things went down the last time you and I met, I mean."

The last time he and I met. Instantly I was transported in my mind's eye back to that long corridor—the one I had seen so often in my dreams. Lined with doors on either side—doors that opened into who-knew-what—it had been like a hallway in a hotel or an office building . . . only this hallway hadn't existed in any hotel or office building known to man. It hadn't even existed in our current dimension.

And Paul had stood there, knowing Jesse and I had no idea how to find our way out of it, and laughed. Just laughed, like it was this big colossal joke that if I didn't return to my own universe soon, I'd die, while Jesse would have been trapped in that hallway forever. I could still hear Paul's laughter ringing in my ears. He had kept on laughing . . . right up until the moment Jesse had slammed a fist into his face.

I could hardly believe any of this was happening. Here it was, a perfectly normal September morning in Carmel, California—which meant, of course, a thick layer of mist hung over everything but would soon burn off to reveal cloudless blue skies and a golden sun—and I was standing there in the breezeway of the Junipero Serra Mission

Academy, face-to-face with the person who'd been haunting my nightmares for weeks.

Only this wasn't a nightmare. I was awake. I knew I was awake, because I would never have dreamed of my friends CeeCee and Adam sauntering by while I was confronting this monster from my past, and going, "Hey, Suze," like it was . . . well, like it was simply the first day back at school after summer vacation.

"You mean the part where you tried to kill me?" I croaked, when CeeCee and Adam were out of earshot. This time, I know he heard my voice shake. I know because he looked perturbed—though maybe it was because of the accusation. In any case, he reached up and dragged one of those largish tanned hands through his curly hair.

"I never tried to kill you, Suze," he said, sounding a little hurt.

I laughed. I couldn't help it. My heart was in my throat, but I laughed anyway. "Oh," I said. "Right."

"I mean it, Suze," he said. "It wasn't like that. I'm just . . . I'm just not very good at losing, you see."

I stared at him. No matter what he told himself, he *had* tried to kill me. But worse, he'd done his best to eliminate Jesse, in a completely underhanded manner. And now he was trying to pass the whole thing off as bad sportsmanship?

"I don't get it," I said, shaking my head. "What did you lose? You didn't lose anything."

"Didn't I, Suze?" His gaze bore into mine. His voice was the one I'd been hearing over and over in my dreams—laughing at me as I struggled to find my way out of a dark, mist-filled hallway at either end of which was a precipice dropping off into a black void of utter nothingness, over which, right before I woke up, I teetered dangerously. It was a voice filled with hidden meaning. . . .

Only I had no idea what that meaning could be, or what he was implying. All I knew was that this guy terrified me.

"Suze," he said with a smile. Smiling—and probably even scowling, too—he looked like a Calvin Klein underwear model. And not just his face, either. I had, after all, seen him in a pair of swim trunks.

"Look, don't be this way," he said. "It's a new school year. Can't we make a new start?"

"No," I said, glad that my voice didn't shake this time. "We can't. In fact, you—you'd better stay away from me."

He seemed to find this deeply amusing. "Or what?" he asked, with another one of those smiles that revealed all of his white, even teeth—a politician's smile, I realized.

"Or you'll regret it," I said, the tremor back in my voice.

"Oh," he said, his dark eyes widening in mock terror. "You'll sic your boyfriend on me?"

It wasn't something I'd have joked around about, if I were him. Jesse could—and probably would, if he found out the guy was back—kill him. Except that I wasn't exactly Jesse's girlfriend, so it wasn't really his job to protect me from creeps like the one in front of me.

He must have figured out from my expression that all was not copacetic in Suze-and-Jesse-land, since he laughed and said, "So that's how it is. Well, I never really thought Jesse was your type, you know. You need someone a little less—"

He didn't get a chance to finish his sentence, because at that moment, CeeCee, who'd been following Adam in the direction of his locker—even though we'd solemnly sworn to each other the night before over the phone that we were not going to start off the new school year chasing boys—came back toward us, her gaze on the guy standing so close to me.

"Suze," she said politely. Unlike me, CeeCee had spent her summer working in the non-profit sector, and so had not had a lot of money to blow on a back-to-school wardrobe and makeover. Not that CeeCee would ever spend her money on anything so frivolous as makeup. Which was a good thing, since, being an albino, she had to special-order all of her makeup anyway, and couldn't just stroll on up to the M.A.C. counter and plunk her money down the way anybody else could.

"Who's your friend?" she wanted to know.

I was not about to stand there and make introductions. In fact, I was seriously thinking of heading to the administrative office and asking just what they were thinking, admitting a guy like this into what I had once considered a passably good school.

But he thrust one of those cool, strong hands at CeeCee and said with that grin that I had once found disarming but that now chilled me to the bone, "Hi. I'm Paul. Paul Slater. Nice to meet you."

Paul Slater. Not really the kind of name to strike terror into the heart of a young girl, huh? I mean, it sounded innocuous enough. *Hi, I'm Paul Slater.* There was nothing in that statement that could have alerted CeeCee to the truth: Paul

Slater was sick, manipulative, and had icicles where his heart should have been.

No, CeeCee had no clue. Because I hadn't told her, of course. I hadn't told anyone.

The more fool I.

If CeeCee found his fingers a little too cold for her liking, she didn't let on.

"CeeCee Webb," she said, as she pumped his hand in her typically businesslike manner. "You must be new here, because I've never seen you around before."

Paul blinked, bringing attention to his eyelashes, which were really long, for a guy's. They looked almost heavy on his eyelids, like they'd be an effort to lift. My stepbrother Jake has sort of the same thing going, only on him, it just makes him look drowsy. On Paul, it had more of a sexy rock-star effect. I glanced worriedly at CeeCee. She was one of the most sensible people I had ever met, but are any of us really immune to the sexy rock-star type?

"My first day," Paul said with another one of those grins. "Lucky for me, I already happen to be acquainted with Ms. Simon here."

"How fortuitous," CeeCee, who, as editor of the school paper, liked big words, said, her white-blond eyebrows raised slightly. "Did you used to go to Suze's old school?"

"No," I said quickly. "He didn't. Look, we better get to homeroom, or we're going to get into trouble. . . ."

But Paul wasn't worried about getting into trouble. Probably because Paul was used to causing it.

"Suze and I had a thing this past summer," he informed CeeCee, whose purple eyes widened behind the lenses of her glasses at this information.

"A *thing*?" she echoed.

"There was no thing," I hastened to assure her. "Believe me. No thing at all."

CeeCee's eyes got even wider. It was clear she didn't believe me. Well, why should she? I was her best friend, it was true. But had I ever once been completely honest with her? No. And she clearly knew it.

"Oh, so you guys broke up?" she asked pointedly.

"No, we didn't break up," Paul said, with another one of those secretive, knowing smiles.

Because we were never going out, I wanted to shriek. You think I'd ever go out with *him*? He's not what you think, CeeCee. He *looks* human, but underneath that studly façade, he's a . . . a . . .

Well, I didn't know what Paul was, exactly.

But then, what did that make me? Paul and I had far more in common than I was comfortable admitting, even to myself.

Even if I'd had the guts to say something along those lines in front of him, I didn't get a chance because suddenly a stern, "Miss Simon! Miss Webb! Haven't you ladies got a class you should be getting to?" rang out.

Sister Ernestine—whose three-month absence from my life had not rendered her any less intimidating, with her enormous chest and even bigger crucifix adorning it—came barreling down upon us, the wide black sleeves of her habit trailing behind her like wings.

"Get going," she tut-tutted us, waving her hands in the direction of our lockers, built into the adobe walls all along the mission's beautifully manicured inner courtyard. "You'll be late to first period."

We got going . . . but unfortunately Paul followed directly behind us.

"Suze and I go way back," he was saying to CeeCee, as we moved along the porticoed hallway toward my locker. "We met at the Pebble Beach Hotel and Golf Resort."

I could only stare at him as I fumbled with the

combination to my locker. I couldn't believe this was happening. I really couldn't. What was Paul doing here? What was Paul doing here enrolling in my school, making my world—from which I'd thought I'd rid him forever—a real-life nightmare?

I didn't want to know. Whatever his motives for coming back, I didn't want to know. I just wanted to get away from him, get to class, anywhere, anywhere at all . . .

. . . so long as it was away from him.

"Well," I said, slamming my locker door closed. I hardly knew what I was doing. I had reached in and blindly grabbed the first books my fingers touched. "Gotta go. Homeroom calls."

He looked down at the books in my arms, the ones I was holding almost as a shield, as if they would protect me from whatever it was—and I was sure there was something—he had in store for me. For us.

"You won't find them in there," Paul said with a cryptic nod at the textbooks bulging from my arms.

I didn't know what he was talking about. I didn't *want* to know. All I knew was that I wanted out of there, and I wanted out of there fast. CeeCee still stood beside me, looking bewilderedly from my face to Paul's. Any second, I knew, she was going to begin to ask questions, questions I didn't dare answer . . . because she wouldn't believe me if I tried.

Still, even though I didn't want to, I heard myself asking, as if the words were being torn involuntarily from my lips, "I won't find what in here?"

"The answers you're looking for." Paul's blue-eyed gaze was intense. "Why you, of all people, were chosen. And what, exactly, you are."

This time, I didn't have to ask what he meant. I knew. I knew as surely as if he'd said the words out loud. He was talking about the gift we shared, he and I, the one over which he seemed to have so much better control—and of which he seemed to have such superior knowledge—than I did.

While CeeCee stood there, staring at the two of us as if we were speaking a foreign language, Paul went on smoothly, "When you're ready to hear the truth about what you are, you'll know where to find me. Because I'll be right here."

And then he walked away, seemingly unaware of all the feminine sighs he drew from my classmates as he moved with pantherlike grace down the breezeway.

Her violet eyes still wide behind her glasses, CeeCee looked up at me wonderingly.

"What," she wanted to know, "was that guy talking about? And who on earth is *Jesse*?"

chapter *two*

I couldn't tell her, of course. I couldn't tell anyone about Jesse, because, frankly, who'd have believed it? I knew only one person—one living person, anyway—who knew the whole truth about people like Paul and me, and that was only because he was one of us. As I sat in front of his mahogany desk a little while later, I couldn't help letting out a groan.

"How could this have happened?" I asked.

Father Dominic, principal of the Junipero Serra Mission Academy, sat behind his enormous desk, looking patient. It was an expression that became the good father, who, rumor had it, grew better looking with every passing year. At nearly sixty-five, he was a white-haired, spectacled Adonis.

He was also very contrite.

"Susannah, I'm sorry. I've been so busy with preparations for the new school year—not to mention the Father Serra festival this coming weekend—I never glanced at the admission rosters." He shook his neatly trimmed white head. "I am so, so sorry."

I grimaced. He was sorry. *He* was sorry? What about *me*? *He* wasn't the one who had to be in the same classes with Paul Slater. Two classes, as a matter of fact: homeroom and U.S. history. Two whole hours a day I was going to have to sit there and look at the guy who'd tried to off my boyfriend and leave me for dead. And that wasn't even counting morning assembly and lunch. That was another hour, right there!

"Although I don't honestly know what I could have done," Father Dom said, rifling through Paul's file, "to prevent his being admitted. His test scores, grades, teacher evaluations . . . everything is exemplary. I am sorry to say that on paper, Paul Slater comes off as a far better student than you did when you first applied to this school."

"You can't tell anything," I pointed out, "about a person's moral fiber from a bunch of test scores." I am a little defensive about this topic, on account of my own test scores having been mediocre enough to have caused the Mission Academy to balk at accepting my application eight months ago when my mother announced we were moving to California so that she could marry Andy Ackerman, the man of her dreams, and now my stepfather.

"No," Father Dominic said, tiredly removing his glasses and cleaning them on the hem of his long black robe. There were, I noticed, purple shadows beneath his eyes. "No, you cannot," he agreed with a deep sigh, placing his wire rims back over the bridge of his perfectly aquiline nose. "Susannah, are you really so certain this boy's motives are less than noble? Perhaps Paul is looking for guidance. It's possible that, with the right influence, he might be made to see the error of his ways. . . ."

"Yeah, Father Dom," I said sarcastically. "And maybe this year I'll get elected Homecoming Queen."

Father Dominic looked disapproving. Unlike me, Father Dominic tended always to think the best of people, at least until their subsequent behavior proved his assumption of their inherent goodness to be wrong. You would think that in the case of Paul Slater, he'd have already seen enough to form a solid basis for judgment on that guy's behalf, but apparently not.

"I am going to assume," Father D. said, "until we've seen something to prove otherwise, that Paul is here at the Mission Academy because he wants to learn. Not just the normal eleventh-grade curriculum, either, Susannah, but what you and I might have to teach him as well. Let us hope that Paul regrets his past actions and truly wishes to make amends. I believe that Paul is here to make a fresh start rather like you did last year, if you'll recall. And it is our duty, as charitable human beings, to help him do just that. Until we learn otherwise, I believe we should give Paul the benefit of the doubt."

I thought this was the worst plan I had ever heard in my life. But the truth was, I didn't have any evidence that Paul was, in fact, here to cause trouble. Not yet, anyway.

"Now," Father D. said, closing Paul's file and leaning back in his chair, "I haven't seen you in a few weeks. How are you, Susannah? And how's Jesse?"

I felt my face heat up. Things were at a sorry pass when the mere mention of Jesse's name could cause me to blush, but there it was.

"Um," I said, hoping Father D. wouldn't notice

my flaming cheeks. "Fine."

"Good," Father Dom said, pushing his glasses up on his nose and looking over at his bookshelf in a distracted manner. "There was a book he mentioned he wanted to borrow—Oh, yes, here it is." Father Dom placed a giant, leatherbound book—it had to have weighed ten pounds at least—in my arms. *Critical Theory Since Plato,* he said with a smile. "Jesse ought to like that."

I didn't doubt it. Jesse liked some of the most boring books known to man. Possibly this was why he wasn't responding to me. I mean, not the way I wanted him to. Because I was not boring enough.

"Very good," Father D. said distractedly. You could tell he had a lot on his mind. Visits from the archbishop always threw him into a tizzy, and this one, for the feast of Father Serra, whom several organizations had been trying unsuccessfully to have made a saint, was going to be a particularly huge pain in the butt, from what I could see.

"Let's just keep an eye on our young friend Mr. Slater," Father Dom went on, "and see how things go. He might very well settle down, Susannah, in a structured environment like the one we offer here at the academy."

I sniffed. I couldn't help it. Father D. really had no idea what he was up against.

"And if he doesn't?" I asked.

"Well," Father Dominic said. "We'll cross that bridge when we get to it. Now run along. You don't want to waste the whole of your lunch break in here with me."

Reluctantly, I left the principal's office, carrying the dusty old tome he'd given me. The morning fog had dispersed, as it always did around eleven, and now the sky overhead was a brilliant blue. In the courtyard, hummingbirds busily worked over the hibiscus. The fountain, surrounded by a half-dozen tourists in Bermuda shorts—the mission, besides being a school, was also a historic landmark and sported a basilica and even a gift shop that were must-sees on any touring bus's schedule—burbled noisily. The deep green fronds of the palm trees waved lazily overhead in the gentle breeze from the sea. It was another gorgeous day in Carmel-by-the-Sea.

So why did I feel so wretched?

I tried to tell myself that I was overreacting. That Father Dom was right—we didn't know what Paul's motives in coming to Carmel were. Perhaps he really had turned over a new leaf.

So why could I not get that image—the one

from my nightmares—out of my head? The long dark hallway and me running through it, looking desperately for a way out, and finding only fog. It was a dream I had nearly once a night, and from which I never failed to wake in a sweat.

Truthfully, I didn't know which was scarier: my nightmare or what was happening now while I was awake. What was Paul doing here? Even more perplexing, how was it that Paul seemed to know so much about the talent he and I shared? There's no newsletter. There are no conferences or seminars. When you put the word *mediator* into any search engine online, all you get is stuff about lawyers and family counselors. I am as clueless now, practically, as I'd been back when I was little and known only that I was . . . well, different from the other kids in my neighborhood.

But Paul. Paul seemed to think he had some kinds of answers.

What could he know about it, though? Even Father Dominic didn't claim to know exactly what we mediators—for lack of a better term— were, and where we'd come from, and just what, exactly, was the extent of our talents . . . and he was older than both of us combined! Sure, we can see and speak to—and even kiss and punch— the dead . . . or rather, the spirits of those who had died and left things untidy, something I'd found out at the age of six, when my dad, who'd passed away from a sudden heart attack, came back for a little post-funeral chat.

But was that it? I mean, was that all mediators were capable of? Not according to Paul.

Despite Father Dominic's assurances that Paul likely meant well, I could not be so sure. People like Paul did not do anything without good reason. So what was he doing back in Carmel? Could it be merely that, now that he'd discovered Father Dom and me, he wished to continue the relationship out of some kind of longing to be with his own kind?

It was possible. Of course, it's equally possible that Jesse really does love me and is just pretending he doesn't, since a romantic relationship between the two of us really wouldn't be all that kosher. . . .

Yeah. And maybe I really *will* get that Homecoming Queen nomination I've been longing for. . . .

I was still trying not to think about this at lunch—the Paul thing, not the Homecoming Queen thing—when, sandwiched on an outdoor bench between Adam and CeeCee, I cracked the pull tab on a can of diet soda and then nearly choked on my first swallow after CeeCee went, "So, spill. Who's this Jesse guy anyway? Answer please this time."

Soda went everywhere, mostly out of my nose. Some of it got on my Benetton sweater set.

CeeCee was completely unsympathetic. "It's diet," she said. "It won't stain. So how come we haven't met him?"

"Yeah," Adam said, getting over his initial mirth at seeing soda come out of my nostrils. "And how come this Paul guy knows him, and we don't?"

Dabbing myself with a napkin, I glanced in Paul's direction. He was sitting on a bench not too far away, surrounded by Kelly Prescott and the other popular people in our class, all of whom were laughing uproariously at some story he'd just told them.

"Jesse's just a guy," I said, because I had a feeling I wasn't going to be able to get away with brushing their questions off. Not this time.

"Just a guy," CeeCee repeated. "Just a guy you are apparently going out with, according to this Paul."

"Well," I said uncomfortably. "Yeah. I guess I am. Sort of. I mean . . . it's complicated."

Complicated? My relationship with Jesse made

Critical Theory Since Plato look like *The Poky Little Puppy*.

"So," CeeCee said, crossing her legs and nibbling contentedly from a bag of baby carrots in her lap. "Tell. Where'd you two meet?"

I could not believe I was actually sitting there, discussing Jesse with my friends. My friends whom I'd worked so hard to keep in the dark about him.

"He, um, lives in my neighborhood," I said. No point in telling them the absolute truth.

"He go to RLS?" Adam wanted to know, referring to Robert Louis Stevenson School and reaching over me to grab a carrot from the bag in CeeCee's lap.

"Um," I said. "Not exactly."

"Don't tell me he goes to Carmel High." CeeCee's eyes widened.

"He's not in high school anymore," I said, since I knew that, given CeeCee's nature, she'd never rest until she knew all. "He, um, graduated already."

"Whoa," CeeCee said. "An older man. Well, no wonder you're keeping him a secret. So, what is he, in college?"

"Not really," I said. "He's, uh, taking some time off. To kind of . . . find himself."

"Hmph." Adam leaned back against the bench and closed his eyes, letting the strong midday sun caress his face. "A slacker. You can do better, Suze. What you need is a guy with a good solid work ethic. A guy like . . . Hey, I know. Me!"

CeeCee, who had had her eye on Adam for as long as I'd known them both, ignored him.

"How long have you guys been going out?" she wanted to know.

"I don't know," I said, feeling pretty miserable now. "It's all sort of new. I mean, I've known him for a while, but the whole dating angle of it . . . that's new. And it isn't really . . . Well, I don't really like to talk about it."

"Talk about what?" A shadow loomed over our bench. Squinting, I looked up and saw my younger stepbrother, David, standing there, his red hair glowing like a halo in the hot sun.

"Nothing," I said, quickly.

Out of everyone in my family—and yes, I did think of the Ackermans, my stepdad and his sons, as part of my family now, the little family that used to be made up of just my mom and me after my dad died—thirteen-year-old David was the one closest to knowing the truth about me. That I wasn't the merely somewhat discontented teenaged girl I pretended to be, that is.

What's more, David knew about Jesse. Knew, and yet didn't know. Because while he, like everyone in the house, had noticed my sudden mood swings and mysterious absence from the family room every night, he could not even begin to imagine what was behind it all.

Now he stood in front of our bench—which was pretty daring, since the upperclassmen did not tend to take kindly to eighth graders like David coming over to what they considered their side of the assembly yard—trying to look like he belonged there, which, considering his hundred-pound frame, braces, and sticky-out ears, could not have been further from the truth.

"Did you see this?" he asked now, shoving a piece of paper beneath my nose.

I took the paper from him. It turned out to be a flyer advertising a hot tub party at 99 Pine Crest Drive on this coming Friday night. Guests were invited to bring a swimsuit if they wanted to have some "hot 'n' frothy fun." Or if they chose to forsake a suit, that was all right, particularly if they happened to be of the female persuasion.

There was a crude drawing on the flyer of a tipsy-looking girl with large breasts downing a can of beer.

"No, you can't go," I said, handing the flyer

back to David with a snort. "You're too young. And somebody ought to show this to your class adviser. Eighth graders shouldn't be having parties like this."

CeeCee, who'd taken the flyer from David's hands, went, "Um, Suze."

"Seriously," I continued. "And I'm surprised at you, David. I thought you were smarter than that. Nothing good ever comes from parties like that. Sure, some people will have fun. But ten to one somebody will end up having to get his stomach pumped or drown or crack his head open or something. It's always fun until someone gets hurt."

"Suze." CeeCee held the flyer up in front of my face just inches from my nose. "Ninety-nine Pine Crest Drive. That's your house, isn't it?"

I snatched the flyer away from her with a gasp. "David! What can you be thinking?"

"It wasn't me," David cried, his already wobbly voice going up another two or three octaves. "Somebody showed it to me in social studies. Brad's passing them around. Some of the seventh graders got some, even—"

I narrowed my eyes in my stepbrother Brad's direction. He was leaning against the basketball pole, trying to look cool, which was pretty hard for a guy whose cerebral cortex was coated, as far as I could tell, with WD-40.

"Excuse me," I said, standing up. "I have to go commit a murder." Then I stalked across the basketball court, the bright orange flyer in my hand.

Brad saw me coming. I noted the look of naked panic that flitted across his features as his gaze fell upon what I had in my hand. He straightened up and tried to run, but I was too quick for him. I cornered him by the drinking fountain and held the flyer up so that he could see it.

"Do you really think," I asked, calmly, "that Mom and Andy are going to allow you to have this . . . this . . . whatever it is?"

The panic on Brad's face had turned to defiance. He stuck out his chin and said, "Yeah, well, what they don't know isn't going to hurt them."

"Brad," I said. Sometimes I felt sorry for him. I really did. He was just such a doofus. "Don't you think they're going to notice when they look out their bedroom window and see a bunch of naked girls in their new hot tub?"

"No," Brad said. "'Cause they aren't going to be around Friday night. Dad's got that guest lecture thing up in San Francisco, and your mom's going with him, remember?"

No, I did not remember. In fact, I wondered if

I had ever even been told. I had been spending a lot of time up in my room lately, it was true, but so much that I'd missed something as important as our parents going away for an entire night? I didn't think so. . . .

"And you better not tell them," Brad said with an unexpected burst of venom, "or you'll be sorry."

I looked at him like he was nuts. "*I'll* be sorry?" I said with a laugh. "Um, excuse me, Brad, but if your dad finds out about this party you're planning, *you're* the one who's going to be grounded for the rest of your life, not me."

"Nuh-uh," Brad said. The look of defiance had been replaced by an even less attractive one of something that was almost venal. "'Cause if you even think about saying anything, I'll tell them about the guy you've been sneaking into your room every night."

chapter *three*

Detention.

That's what you get at the Junipero Serra Mission Academy when you sucker punch your stepbrother on school grounds and a teacher happens to notice.

"I can't understand what came over you, Suze," said Mrs. Elkins, who, in addition to teaching ninth- and tenth-grade biology, was also in charge of staying after school with juvenile delinquents like me. "And on the first day back, too. Is this how you want to start out the new year?"

But Mrs. Elkins didn't understand. And I couldn't exactly tell her or anything. I mean, how could I tell her that it had all just suddenly become too much? That discovering that my stepbrother knew something I had struggled to hide from the rest of my family for months now—on top of finding out that a monster from my dreams was currently stalking the halls of my own school in the guise of an Abercrombie and Fitch–wearing hottie—had caused me to melt down like a Maybelline lipstick left in the sun?

I couldn't tell her. I merely took my punishment in silence, watching the minutes on the clock drag slowly by. Neither I nor any of the other prisoners would be released until four o'clock.

"I hope," Mrs. Elkins said when that hour finally arrived, "that you've learned a lesson, Suze. You aren't setting a very good example for the younger children, now, are you, brawling on school grounds like that?"

Me? I wasn't setting a good example? What about Brad? Brad was the one who was planning to have his own personal Oktoberfest in our living room. And yet Brad had *me* by the short hairs. And did he ever know it.

"Yeah," he'd said to me at lunch, when I'd stood there staring at him in utter dumbfoundedness, unable to believe what I'd just heard. "Think you're so slick, don't you, letting the guy sneak up into your room every night, huh? How's he get in, anyway? That bay window of yours, the one over the porch roof? Well, I guess your little secret's blown now, huh? So you just keep quiet about my party, and I'll keep quiet about this Jesse guy."

I'd been so flabbergasted by this news that Brad could hear—had heard—Jesse, I hadn't been able to formulate a coherent sentence for several minutes, during which time Brad exchanged greetings with various members of his posse who came up to high-five him and say things like, "Dude! Tub time. I'm so there."

Finally, I managed to unlock my jaw and demanded, "Oh, yeah? Well, what about Jake? I mean, Jake's not going to let you have a bunch of your friends over to get wasted."

Brad just looked at me like I was nuts. "Are you kidding?" he asked. "Who do you think's providing the beer? Jake's gonna steal me a keg from where he works."

I narrowed my eyes at him. "*Jake? Jake's* getting *you* beer? No way. He would never—" Then comprehension dawned. "How much are you paying him?"

"A hundred big ones," Brad said. "Exactly half of what he's shy on that Camaro he's been wanting."

There was little Jake wouldn't do to get his

hands on a Camaro all his own, I knew.

Stymied, I stared at him some more. "What about David?" I asked, finally. "David's going to tell."

"No, he isn't," Brad said confidently. "'Cause if he does, I'll kick his bony butt from here to Anchorage. And you better not try to defend him, either, or your mom's gonna get a big fat helping of Jesse pie."

That's when I hit him. I couldn't help it. It was like my fist had a mind of its own. One minute it was at my side, and the next it was sinking into Brad's gut.

The fight was over in a second. A half second, even. Mr. Gillarte, the new track coach, pulled us apart before Brad had a chance to get in a blow of his own.

"Walk it off," he ordered me with a shove, while he bent to tend a frantically gasping Brad.

So I walked it off. Right up to Father D., who was standing in the courtyard, supervising the stringing of fairy lights around the trunk of a palm tree.

"What can I tell you, Susannah?" he'd said, sounding exasperated when I was finished explaining the situation. "Some people are more perceptive than others."

"Yeah, but *Brad*?" I had to keep my voice down because a bunch of the gardeners were around, all helping to set up the decorations for the feast of Father Serra, which was happening on Saturday, the day after Brad's hot tub bacchanal.

"Well, Susannah," Father D. said. "You couldn't have expected to keep Jesse a secret forever. Your family was bound to find out sometime."

Maybe. What I couldn't fathom was how Brad, of all people, knew about him when some of my more intelligent family members—like Andy, for instance, or my mom—were totally clueless.

On the other hand, Max, the family dog, had always known about Jesse—wouldn't go near my room because of him. And on an intellectual level, Brad and Max had a lot in common . . . though Max was a little bit smarter, of course.

"I sincerely hope," Mrs. Elkins said, when she'd released me and my fellow prisoners at last, "that I won't see you here again this year, Suze."

"You and me both, Mrs. E.," I'd replied, gathering my things. Then I'd bolted.

Outside, it was a clear, hot September afternoon in northern California, which meant that the sun was blinding, the sky was so blue it hurt to look at it, and off in the distance, you could see the white surf of the Pacific as it curled up against Carmel Beach. I had missed all of my possible rides home—Adam, who was still eager to take anyone anywhere in his sporty green VW Bug, and of course Brad, who'd inherited the Land Rover from Jake, who now drove a beat-up Honda Civic but only until he obtained his dream car—and it was a two-mile walk to 99 Pine Crest Drive. Mostly uphill.

I'd gotten as far as the gates of the school before my knight in shining armor showed up. At least, that's what I suppose he thought he was. He wasn't on any milk-white palfrey though. He drove a silver BMW convertible, the top already conveniently lowered. It so figured.

"Come on," he said, as I stood in front of the mission, waiting for the traffic light to change so I could cross the busy highway. "Get in. I'll give you a ride home."

"No, thank you," I said lightly. "I prefer to walk."

"Suze." Paul looked bored. "Just get in the car."

"No," I said. See, I had fully learned my lesson, insofar as the whole getting-into-cars-with-guys-who'd-once-tried-to-kill-me thing went. And it wasn't going to happen again. Especially not with Paul, who'd not only once tried to kill me but who had frightened me so thoroughly while doing it that I continually relived the incident in my dreams. "I told you. I'm walking."

Paul shook his head, laughing to himself. "You really are," he said, "a piece of work."

"Thank you." The light changed, and I started across the intersection. I knew it well. I did not need an escort.

But that's exactly what I got. Paul drove right alongside me, clocking a grand total of about two miles per hour.

"Are you going to follow me all the way home?" I inquired as we started up the steep incline that gave the Carmel hills their name. It was a good thing that this particular road was not highly trafficked at four in the afternoon, or Paul just might have made some of my neighbors mad, clogging up the only pathway to civilization the way he was driving.

"Yes," Paul said. "That is, unless you'll stop acting like such a brat and get into the car."

"No, thanks," I said again.

I kept walking. It was hot out. I was beginning to feel a little moist in my sweater set. But no way was I going to get into that guy's car. I trudged along the side of the road, careful to avoid any plants that resembled my deadliest of enemies—before Paul had come along, anyway—poison oak, and silently cursed *Critical Theory Since Plato*, which seemed to be growing heavier and heavier in my arms with every step.

"You're wrong not to trust me," Paul remarked as he slithered up the hill alongside me in his silver snakemobile. "We're the same, you and I, you know."

"I sincerely hope that isn't true," I said. I have often found that with some enemies, politeness can be as strong a deterrent as a fist. I'm not kidding. Try it some time.

"Sorry to disappoint you," Paul said. "But it is. What'd Father Dominic tell you, anyway? He tell you not to spend any time alone with me? Not to believe a word I say?"

"Not at all," I said in the same distant tone. "Father Dominic thinks I should give you the benefit of the doubt."

Paul, behind his leather-covered steering wheel, looked surprised. "Really? He said that?"

"Oh, yes," I said, noticing a beautiful clump of buttercups growing alongside the road, and carefully skirting them in case they hid any dangerous stalks of poison oak. "Father Dominic thinks you're here because you want to bond with the only other mediators you know. He thinks it's our duty as charitable human beings to allow you to make amends and help you along the path to righteousness."

"But you don't agree with him?" Paul was staring at me intently. Well, and why not? Considering how slowly he was going, it wasn't like he had to keep an eye on the road or anything.

"Look," I said, wishing I had a barrette or something I could put my hair up with. It was beginning to stick to the back of my neck. The tortoiseshell hair clip I had started out with that morning had mysteriously disappeared. "Father Dominic is the nicest person I have ever met. All he lives for is to help others. He genuinely believes that human beings are, by nature, good, and that, if treated as such, will respond accordingly."

"But you," Paul said, "don't agree, I take it?"

"I think we both know that Father Dom is living in a dreamworld." I looked straight ahead as I trudged up the hill, hoping that Paul wouldn't guess that my staggering heartbeat had nothing to do with the exercise and everything to do with his presence. "But because I don't want to let the guy down, I'm going to keep my personal opinion about you—that you're a user and a psychopath—to myself."

"A psychopath?" Paul seemed delighted to hear

himself described this way . . . further proof that he was, in fact, exactly what I thought him. "I like the sound of that. I've been called a lot of things before but never a psychopath."

"It wasn't a compliment," I felt compelled to point out, since he seemed to be taking it that way.

"I know," he said. "That's what makes it so particularly amusing. You're quite a girl, you know that?"

"Whatever," I said, irritated. I couldn't even seem to insult the guy successfully. "Just tell me one thing."

"Name it," he said.

"That night we ran into each other"—I pointed toward the sky—"you know, up there?"

He nodded. "Yeah. What about it?"

"How'd you get there? I mean, nobody exorcised you, right?"

Paul was grinning now. I saw, to my dismay, that I'd asked him exactly the question he'd most wanted to hear.

"No, nobody exorcised me," he said. "And you didn't need anybody to exorcise you, either."

This came close to flooring me. I froze in my tracks. "Are you trying to tell me that I can just go strolling around up there whenever I want?" I asked him, truly stunned.

"There's a lot," Paul said, still grinning lazily, "that you can do that you haven't figured out yet, Suze. Things you've never dreamed of. Things I can show you."

The silky tone of his voice didn't fool me. Paul was a charmer, it was true, but he was also deadly.

"Yeah," I said, praying that he couldn't see how fast my heart was beating through all that pink silk. "I'm sure."

"I'm serious, Suze," Paul said. "Father Dominic is a great guy. I'm not denying it. But he's just a mediator. You're a little something more."

"I see." I hitched my shoulders and started walking again. We had reached the crest of the hill finally, and I entered some shade afforded by the giant pine trees on either side of the road. My relief at finally being out of the heat was palpable. I only wished I could rid myself of Paul as easily. "So all my life, people have been telling me I'm one thing, and all of a sudden you come along, and you say I'm something else, and I'm just supposed to believe you?"

"Yes," Paul said.

"Because you're such a trustworthy person," I quipped, sounding a lot more self-assured than I actually felt.

"Because I'm all you've got," he corrected me.

"Well, that's not a real whole lot, is it?" I glared at him. "Or do I need to point out that the last time I saw you, you left me stranded in hell?"

"It wasn't hell," Paul said, with another one of his trademark eyerolls. "And you'd have found your way out eventually."

"What about Jesse?" I demanded. My heart was beating more loudly than ever, because this, of course, was what really mattered—not what he'd done, or tried to do to me—but what he'd done to Jesse . . . what I was terrified he'd try to do again.

"I said I was sorry about that." Paul sounded irritated. "Besides, it all turned out okay in the end, didn't it? It's like I told you, Suze. You're much more powerful than you know. You just need someone to show you your true potential. You need a mentor—a real one, not a sixty-year-old priest who thinks Father Junipero Whoever is the be-all and end-all of the universe."

"Right," I said. "And I suppose you think you're just the guy to play Mr. Miyagi to my Karate Kid."

"Something like that."

We were rounding the corner to 99 Pine Crest Drive, perched on a hill overlooking Carmel Valley. My room, at the front of the house, had an ocean view. At night, fog blew in from the sea, and you could almost see it falling in misty tendrils over the sills if I left my windows open. It was a nice house, one of the oldest in Carmel, a former boardinghouse, circa 1850. It didn't even have a reputation for being haunted.

"What do you say, Suze?" Paul had one arm flung casually across the back of the empty passenger seat beside him. "Dinner tonight? My treat? I'll tell you things about yourself—about what you are—that no one else on this planet knows."

"Thanks," I said, stepping off the road and into my pine-needle-strewn yard, feeling insanely relieved. Well, and why not? I had survived an encounter with Paul Slater without being hurled into another plane of existence. That was quite an accomplishment. "But no thanks. See you in school tomorrow."

Then I waded through the heavy carpet of pine needles to my driveway, while behind me, I heard Paul calling, "Suze! Suze, wait!"

Only I didn't wait. I went straight up the driveway to the front porch, climbed the steps, then opened the front door and went inside.

I did not look back. I did not look back even once.

"I'm home," I called, in case there was anybody

downstairs who particularly cared. There was. I found myself being interrogated by my stepfather, who was cooking dinner and seemed anxious to know all about "my day." After telling him, then seizing sustenance from the kitchen in the form of an apple and a diet soda, I climbed the steps to the second floor, and flung open the door to my room.

There was a ghost sitting there on the windowsill. He looked up when I walked in.

"Hello," Jesse said.

chapter *four*

I didn't tell Jesse about Paul.

I probably should have. There were a lot of things I probably should have told Jesse, but hadn't exactly gotten around to yet.

Except I knew what would happen if I did: Jesse would want to rush into some big confrontation with the guy, and all that would result in was somebody getting exorcised again . . . that somebody being Jesse. And I really didn't think I could take it. Not that. Not again.

So I kept Paul's sudden matriculation at the Mission Academy to myself. I mean, things were weird between Jesse and me, it was true. But that didn't mean I was at all anxious to lose him.

"So how was school?" Jesse wanted to know.

"Fine," I said. I was afraid to say anything more. For one thing, I was worried I might start blabbing about Paul. And for another, well, I'd found that the less said between Jesse and me, overall, the better. Otherwise, I had a tendency to prattle nervously. While I'd found that generally, prattling kept Jesse from dematerializing—as he tended to do more often now, with a hasty apology, whenever any awkward silences ensued between us—it did not seem to engender a similar desire to gab from him. Jesse had been almost unbearably quiet since . . .

Well, since the day we'd kissed.

I don't know what it is about guys that makes them French you one day, then act like you don't exist the next. But that was the treatment I had been getting from Jesse lately. I mean, not three weeks ago he had pulled me into his arms and laid a kiss on me that I had felt all the way down to the base of my spine. I had melted in his embrace, thinking that at last, at long last, I could reveal to him my true feelings, the secret love I had borne him since the minute—well, almost, anyway—I had first walked into my new bedroom and found it already occupied. Never mind that that occupant had breathed his last over a century and a half ago.

I should, I suppose, have known better than to fall in love with a ghost. But that's the thing about us mediators. To us, ghosts have as much matter as anyone living. Except for the whole immortal thing, there was no reason in the world why Jesse and I, if we wanted to, couldn't have the torrid affair I'd been dreaming of since he'd first resolutely refused to call me anything but my full name, Susannah, the name no one else but Father Dom ever used.

Except that no torrid affair followed. After that first kiss—which had been interrupted by my youngest stepbrother—there'd been no other. Jesse had, in fact, apologized profusely for it, then seemed purposefully to avoid me—though I had made it a point to let him know that the whole thing had been all right . . . more than all right . . . by me.

Now I couldn't help wondering if maybe I'd been too accommodating. Jesse probably thought I was easy or something. I mean, back when he'd been alive, ladies slapped men who'd been as forward as he had been. Even men who looked like Jesse, with flashing dark eyes, thick black hair, washboard abs, and irresistibly sexy smiles.

I still find it hard to believe anybody could have hated a guy like that enough to off him, but that's exactly how Jesse ended up haunting my bedroom, the room he was strangled to death in a hundred and fifty years ago.

Given the circumstances, I really didn't think there was much point in telling Jesse the details about my day. I just handed him *Critical Theory Since Plato* and said, "Father Dominic says hello."

Jesse seemed pleased by the book. Just my luck to be in love with a guy who gets more jazzed by critical theory than he seems to by the idea of my tongue in his mouth.

Jesse thumbed through the book while I poured the contents of my backpack on my bed. I was weighted down with homework already, and it was only the first day back. I could tell that eleventh grade was going to be just jam-packed with fun and adventure. I mean, between Paul Slater and trig, what could be more exciting?

I should have said something to Jesse about Paul then. I should have just been like, "Hey, guess what? Remember that Paul guy whose nose you tried to break? Yeah, he goes to my school now."

Because if I'd just been all casual about it, maybe it wouldn't have been a big deal. I mean, yeah, Jesse hated the guy—and with good reason. But I could have downplayed the whole fact that Paul might possibly be Satan's spawn. I mean, the guy *does* sport a Fossil watch. How malevolent could he be?

But just as I was kind of getting the guts up to go, "Oh, yeah, and that Paul Slater dude, remember him? He showed up in my homeroom this morning," Brad shrieked up the stairs that dinner was ready.

Since my stepdad has this big thing about all of us gathering as a family at mealtimes and breaking bread together, I was forced to leave Jesse's side at that point—not that he seemed to care—and go downstairs and actually converse with the household . . . a major sacrifice, considering what I could be doing instead: making myself available for more kisses from the man of my dreams.

Tonight, however, like most nights, didn't look as if it was going to yield any passionate embraces, so I went glumly down the stairs. Andy had prepared steak fajitas, one of his best dishes. I had to give my mother credit for finding a guy who was not only handy around the house but who was also practically a gourmet cook. Given that my mom and I had basically lived on takeout food back before she'd remarried, this was definitely an improvement.

The fact, however, that Mr. Fix-It had come with three teenaged sons? That part I was still sort of iffy about.

Brad burped as I entered the dining room. Only he had mastered the art of burping words. The word he burped as I walked in was *"Loser."*

"You're one to talk," was my witty rejoinder.

"Brad," Andy said severely. "Go and get the sour cream, please."

Rolling his eyes, Brad slid out from his place at the table and trudged back into the kitchen.

"Hi, Susie," my mother said, coming up and ruffling my hair affectionately. "How was your first day back?"

Only my mother, out of all the human beings on the planet, is allowed to call me Susie. Fortunately I had already made this abundantly clear to my stepbrothers, so that they did not even snicker when she did it anymore.

I didn't feel it would have been appropriate to have answered my mother's question truthfully. After all, she is unaware of the fact that her only child is a liaison between the living and the dead. She is not acquainted with Paul, or with the fact that he once tried to kill me, nor is she aware of the existence of Jesse. My mother merely thinks that I am a late bloomer, a wallflower who will come into her own soon enough, and then have boyfriends to spare. Which is surprisingly naïve for a woman who works as a television news journalist, even if it is only for a local affiliate.

Sometimes I envy my mom. It must be nice to live on her planet.

"My day was all right," was how I responded to my mother's question.

"'S not going to be so good tomorrow," Brad pointed out, as he came back with the sour cream.

My mother had taken her seat at one end of the table and was flipping out her napkin. We use only cloth napkins. Another Andy-ism. It is more ecologically responsible and makes the presentation of the meal way more Martha Stewart.

"Really?" Mom said, her eyebrows, dark as mine, rose. "How so?"

"Tomorrow's when we give the nominations for student body government," Brad said, sliding back into his place. "And Suze is going down as VP."

Flipping out my own napkin and laying it delicately across my lap—along with the giant head of Max, the Ackermans' dog, who spent every meal with his muzzle resting on my thigh, waiting for whatever might fall from my fork and into my lap, a practice I was now so used to, I hardly even noticed anymore—I said, in response to my mother's questioning gaze, "I have no idea what he's talking about."

Brad looked innocent. "Kelly didn't catch you after school?"

Not exactly, given that I'd been in detention after school, something Brad knew perfectly well. He intended to torture me about it for a while though, you could tell.

"No," I said. "Why?"

"Well, Kel's already asked someone else to be her running mate this year. That new guy, Paul Whatsit." Brad shrugged his shoulders, from which his thick wrestler's neck sprouted like a tree trunk from between a couple of boulders. "So I guess Suze's reign as VP is *finito*."

My mother glanced at me, concernedly. "You didn't know about this, Susie?"

It was my turn to shrug. "No," I said. "But it's cool. I never really thought of myself as the student government type."

This reply did not have the desired effect, however. My mother pressed her lips together, then said, "Well, I don't like it. Some new boy coming in and taking Susie's place. It isn't fair."

"It may not be fair," David pointed out, "but it's

the natural order of things. Darwin proved that the strongest and fittest of the species tend to be the most successful, and Paul Slater is a superb physical specimen. Every female who comes in contact with him, I've noticed, has a distinct propensity to exhibit preening behavior."

My mother heard this last comment with some amusement. "My goodness," she said mildly. "And you, Susie? Does Paul Slater cause you to exhibit preening behavior?"

"Hardly," I said.

Brad burped again. This time when he did it, he said, "*Liar.*"

I glared at him. "Brad," I said. "I do *not* like Paul Slater."

"That's not what it looked like to me," Brad said, "when I saw the two of you in the breezeway this morning."

"Wrong," I said hotly. "You could not be more wrong."

"Oh," Brad said. "Give it up, Suze. There was definite preenage going on. Unless you just had so much mousse in your hair that your fingers got stuck in there."

"Enough," my mother said, as I drew breath to deny this, too. "Both of you."

"I do not like Paul Slater," I said again, just in

case Brad hadn't heard me the first time. "Okay? In fact, I hate him."

My mother looked aggrieved. "Susie," she said, "I'm surprised at you. It's wrong to say you hate anyone. And how could you hate the poor boy already? You only just met him today."

"She knows him from before," Brad volunteered. "From over the summer at Pebble Beach."

I glared at him some more. "How do *you* know *that*?"

"Paul told me," Brad said with a shrug.

Feeling a sense of dread—it would be just like Paul to spill the whole mediator thing to my family just to mess with me—I asked, trying to sound casual, "Oh, yeah? What else did he tell you?"

"Just that," Brad said. Then his tone grew sarcastic. "Much as it might come as a surprise to you, Suze, people do have other stuff to talk about besides you."

"Brad," Andy said in a warning tone as he came out of the kitchen carrying a tray of sizzling strips of beef and another of soft, steaming tortillas. "Watch it." Then, lowering the twin trays, his gaze fastened on the empty chair beside me. "Where's Jake?"

We all glanced blankly at one another. It hadn't even registered that my eldest stepbrother was missing. None of us knew where Jake was. But all of us knew from Andy's tone that when Jake got home, he was a dead man.

"Maybe," my mother ventured, "he got held up in a class. You know it is only his first week of college, Andy. His schedule may not be the most regular for a while."

"I asked him this morning," Andy said in an aggrieved tone, "if he was going to be home in time for supper, and he said he was. If he was going to be late, the least he could have done was call."

"Maybe he's stuck in some line at registration," my mom said soothingly. "Come on, Andy. You've made a lovely meal. It would be a shame not to sit down and eat it before it gets cold."

Andy sat down, but he didn't look at all eager to eat. "It's just," he said, in a speech we'd all heard approximately four hundred times before, "when someone goes to the trouble to prepare a nice meal, it's only polite that everybody shows up for it on time—"

It was as he was saying this that the front door slammed, and Jake's voice sounded from the foyer: "Keep your shirt on, I'm here." Jake knew his father well.

My mom shot Andy a look over the bowls of

shredded lettuce and cheese we were passing around. The look said, *See. Told you so*.

"Hey," Jake said, coming into the dining room at his usual far-less-than-brisk pace. "Sorry I'm late. Got held up at the bookstore. The lines to buy books were unbelievable."

My mom's told-you-so look deepened.

All Andy did was growl, "You're lucky. This time. Sit down and eat." Then, to Brad, he said, "Pass the salsa."

Except that Jake didn't sit down and eat. Instead, he stood there, one hand in the front pocket of his jeans, the other still dangling his car keys.

"Uh," he said. "Listen . . ."

We all looked up at him, expecting something interesting to happen, like for Jake to say that the pizza place had messed up his schedule again, and that he couldn't stay for dinner. This generally resulted in some major fireworks from Andy.

But instead, Jake said, "I brought a friend with me. Hope that's okay."

Since my stepfather would rather have a thousand people crowded around our dinner table than a single one of us missing from it, he said equally, "Fine, fine. Plenty for everyone. Take another place setting from the counter."

So Jake went to the counter to grab a plate and knife and fork, while his "friend" came slouching into view, having apparently dawdled in the living room, no doubt taken aback by the plethora of family photos my mother had plastered all over the walls there.

Sadly, Jake's friend was not of the feminine variety, so we could not look forward to teasing him about it later. Neil Jankow, as he was introduced, was nevertheless, as David would put it, an interesting specimen. He was well groomed, which set him apart from most of Jake's surf buddies. His jeans did not sag somewhere midway down his thighs but were actually belted properly around his waist, a fact that also put him a cut above most young men his age.

This did not mean, however, that he was a hottie. He wasn't, by any means. He was almost painfully thin, and pasty-skinned as well, and had longish blond hair. Still, I could tell my mother approved of him, since he was excruciatingly polite, calling her ma'am—as in "Thank you very much for letting me stay for dinner, ma'am"— though his implication, that my mother had prepared the meal, was somewhat sexist, since Andy was the one who had done all the cooking.

Still, nobody seemed to take offense, and room

was made for young master Neil at the table. He sat down and, following Jake's lead, began to eat . . . not very heartily but with an appreciation that seemed unfeigned. Neil, we soon learned, was in Jake's Intro to English Literature seminar. Like Jake, Neil was just entering his first year at NoCal—the local slang for Northern California State College. Like Jake, Neil was from the area. His family, in fact, lived in the valley. His father owned a number of restaurants in the area, including one or two at which I had actually eaten. Like Jake, Neil wasn't so sure what he wanted to major in, but, also like Jake, he expected to enjoy college much more than he had high school, since he'd arranged his schedule so that he didn't have a single morning class, and so could spend the A.M. hours sleeping in, or, if he happened to wake before eleven, taking advantage of a few waves over at Carmel Beach before his first class.

By the end of the meal, I had many questions about Neil. I had a big one about one thing in particular. It was something that, I was fairly certain, hadn't bothered anyone besides me. And yet I really felt that I was owed some sort of explanation, at least. Not that I could have said anything about it. Not with so many people around.

That was part of the problem. There were too many people around. And not just the people gathered around the dinner table, either. No, there was the guy who'd come into the room and stood there during the entire course of our meal, right behind Neil's chair, watching him in complete silence, with a baleful look on his face.

This guy, unlike Neil, was good-looking. Dark-haired and cleft-chinned, you could tell that, beneath his Dockers and black Polo, he was cut . . . he'd worked long and hard, I hadn't any doubt, to cultivate those triceps, not to mention what I guessed would be a killer set of washboard abs.

That wasn't the only difference between this guy and Jake's friend Neil, though. There was also the little fact that Neil, to the best of my knowledge, was noticeably alive, while the guy standing behind him was, well . . .

Dead.

chapter *five*

It was so like Jake to bring home a haunted guest.

Not that Neil appeared to know he was being haunted. He seemed perfectly oblivious to the ghostly presence behind him—as was the rest of my family, with the exception of Max. The minute Neil sat down, Max took off for the living room with a whine that caused Andy to shake his head and say, "That dog gets more neurotic every day."

Poor Max. I so know how he felt.

Except that unlike the dog, I couldn't slink from the dining room and go cower in another part of the house, the way I wanted to. I mean, doing so would only engender unnecessary questions.

Besides, I'm a mediator. Dealing with the undead is kind of unavoidable for me.

Though there are definitely times when I wished I could get out of it. Now was one of those times.

Not that I could do anything about it. No, I was stuck at the table, trying to choke down steak fajitas while being stared at by a dead guy, a great end to my already way-less-than-perfect day.

The dead guy, for his part, looked pretty peeved. Well, and why not? I mean, he was *dead*. I had no idea how he'd come to be parted with his soul, but it must have been sudden, because he didn't seem very accustomed to the whole thing yet. Whenever anybody asked to be passed something that was near him, he reached for it . . . only to have it swept out from underneath his ghostly fingers by one of the living at the table. This caused him to look annoyed. But most of his animosity, I noticed, seemed reserved for Neil. Every bite of fajita Jake's new friend took, every chip he dipped into his guacamole, seemed to enrage the dead guy more. His jaw muscles twitched, and his fists tightened convulsively each time Neil replied in his quiet voice, "Yes, ma'am" or "No, ma'am," to any of the many questions my mom put to him.

Finally I couldn't stand it anymore—it was *creepy*, sitting there at the table with this enraged ghost that only I could see . . . and I'm *used* to being stared at by ghosts—so I got up and started clearing everybody's empty plates, even though it was Brad's turn to do it. He gaped at me—providing us all with a very lovely view of some chewed-up steak he still had in his mouth— but didn't say anything about it. I think he was afraid that if he did, it might snap me out of whatever delusion I was under that it was my night to do the dishes. Either that or he figured I was trying to stay in his good graces so he wouldn't tell on me about the "guy" I was entertaining nightly in my room.

Anyway, my getting a move on with the dishes seemed to act as a signal that the meal was over, since everyone else got up and went out onto the deck to look at the new hot tub, which Andy was still showing proudly to every single person who walked through the front door, whether they asked to see it or not. It was while I was in the kitchen rinsing the plates before placing them in the dishwasher that Neil's walking shadow and I ended up alone together. He stood near enough to me—gazing through the sliding glass doors at everybody out on the deck—that I was able to reach out with a sudsy hand and tug on his shirt without anybody noticing.

I startled him pretty badly. He swung around, his gaze furious and yet incredulous at the same time. Clearly, he hadn't been aware that I could see him.

"Hey," I whispered to him, while everybody else was chatting about chlorine and the flan Andy had made for dessert. "You and I should talk."

The guy looked shocked.

"You—you can see me?" he stammered.

"Obviously," I said.

He blinked, then glanced out the sliding glass doors. "But they—they can't?"

"No," I said.

"Why?" he asked. "I mean, why you and not . . . them?"

"Because I'm a mediator," I explained.

He looked blank. "A what?"

"Hang on a sec," I said, because I could see my mother suddenly coming toward the sliding glass doors from the deck.

"Brr," she said, as she pulled the door shut behind her. "It gets cold out there when the sun starts to go down. How are you doing with those dishes, Susie? Do you need any help?"

"Nope," I said, cheerfully. "It's all good."

"Are you sure? I thought it was Brad's turn to clear the table."

"I don't mind," I said with a smile I hoped she didn't notice was completely forced.

It didn't work.

"Susie, honey," she said. "You aren't upset, are you? Over what Brad was saying about this other boy being nominated for vice president in your place?"

"Uh," I said, with a glance at Ghost Boy, who looked pretty annoyed at the interruption. I couldn't really blame him. I guess it *was* kind of unprofessional of me to have a mother-daughter bonding session in the middle of a mediation. "No, not really, Mom. I'm fine with it, actually."

I wasn't lying, either. Not being in the student government this year was going to free up a lot of time for me. Time I had no idea what I was going to do with, of course, since it didn't look as if I'd be spending any of it being lifted to any romantic heights by Jesse. Still, hope springs eternal.

My mom continued to hover in the doorway, looking concerned.

"Well, Susie, honey," she said, "you're going to have to replace it with some other extracurricular, you know. Colleges look for that sort of thing in their applicants. You're less than two years away from graduation. You'll be leaving us soon."

Jeez! My mom didn't even know about Jesse, and she was still doing all she could to keep the two of us apart, unaware that Jesse himself was taking care of that all on his own.

"Fine, Mom," I said, eyeing Ghost Guy uncomfortably. I mean, I wasn't exactly thrilled that he was privy to all this. "I'll join the swim team. Will that make you happy? Having to drive me to five A.M. practices every day?"

"That wasn't even very convincing, Susie," my mom said in a dry voice. "I know perfectly well you'd never join the swim team. You're too obsessed with your hair and what all those pool chemicals might do to it."

And then she drifted off into the living room, leaving Ghost Guy and me alone in the kitchen.

"All right," I said quietly. "Where were we?"

The guy just shook his head. "I still can't believe you can see me," he said in a shocked voice. "I mean, you don't know . . . you can't know what it's been like. It's like everywhere I go, people just look through me."

"Yes," I said, tossing aside the dish towel I'd been using to dry my hands. "That's because you're dead. The question is, what made you that way?"

Ghost Guy seemed taken aback by my tone. I

guess it *was* a little curt. But then, I wasn't having the best day.

"Are you . . ." He eyed me sort of warily. "*Who* did you say you were again?"

"My name's Suze," I told him. "I'm a mediator."

"A *what*?"

"Mediator," I repeated. "It's my job to help the dead pass on to the other side . . . their next life, or whatever. What's your name, anyway?"

Ghost Boy blinked again. "Craig," he said.

"Okay. Well, listen, Craig. Something's screwy, because I highly doubt the cosmos intended for you to be hanging around my kitchen as part of your whole afterlife experience. You have got to move on."

Craig knit his dark brows. "Move on where?"

"Well, that's for you to find out when you get there," I said. "Anyway, the big question isn't where you're going but why you haven't gotten there already."

"You mean . . ." Craig's hazel eyes were wide. "You mean this isn't . . . it?"

"Of course this isn't it," I said, a little amused. "You think after they die, everybody ends up at ninety-nine Pine Crest Drive?"

Craig hitched his broad shoulders. "No. I guess not. It's just that . . . when I woke up, you know,

I didn't know where to go. Nobody could . . . you know. See me. I mean, I went out into the living room, and my mom was crying like she couldn't stop. It was kind of spooky."

He wasn't kidding.

"That's okay," I said, more gently than before. "That's how it happens, sometimes. It's just not normal. Most people do go straight to the next . . . well, phase of their consciousness. You know, to their next life, or to eternal damnation if they screwed up during their last one. That kind of thing." His eyes kind of widened at the words *eternal damnation*, but since I wasn't even sure there was such a thing, I hurried on. "What we've got to figure out now is why you didn't. Move on right away, I mean. Something is obviously holding you back. We need to—"

But at that point, the examination of the hot tub—Andy's precious hot tub, which would, in less than a week from now, be filled with vomit and beer, if Brad's party went on according to plan—ended, and everyone came back inside. I gestured for Craig to follow me, and started up the stairs, where, I felt, we could continue talking uninterrupted.

At least by the living. Jesse, on the other hand, was another story.

"*Nombre de Dios*," he said, startled from the pages of *Critical Theory Since Plato* when I came banging back into my bedroom, Craig close at my heels. Spike, Jesse's cat, arched his back before seeing it was only me—with another of my pesky ghost friends—and settled back up against Jesse.

"Sorry about that," I said. Seeing Jesse's gaze move past me and fasten onto the ghost boy, I made introductions: "Jesse, this is Craig. Craig, Jesse. You two should get along. Jesse's dead, too."

Craig, however, seemed to find the sight of Jesse—who, as usual, was dressed in what had been the height of fashion in the last year he'd been alive, 1850 or so, including knee-high black leather boots, somewhat tight-fitting black trousers, and a big billowy white shirt open at the collar—a bit much. So much, in fact, that Craig had to sit down heavily—or as heavily as someone without any real matter could sit, anyway—on the edge of my bed.

"Are you a pirate?" Craig asked Jesse.

Jesse, unlike me, did not find this very amusing. I guess I can't really blame him.

"No," he said tonelessly. "I'm not."

"Craig," I said, trying to keep a straight face, and failing despite the look Jesse shot me.

"Really, you've got to think. There's got to be a reason why you are still hanging around here instead of off where you're supposed to be. What do you think that reason could be? What's holding you back?"

Craig finally dragged his gaze away from Jesse. "I don't know," he said. "Maybe the fact that I'm not supposed to be dead?"

"Okay," I said, trying to be patient. Because the thing is, of course, everybody thinks this. That they died too young. I've had folks who croaked at age 104 complain to me about the injustice of it all.

But I try to be professional about the whole thing. I mean, mediation is, after all, my job. Not that I get paid for doing it or anything, unless you count, you know, karma-wise. I hope.

"I can certainly see why you might feel that way," I went on. "Was it sudden? I mean, you weren't sick or anything, were you?"

Craig looked indignant. "Sick? Are you kidding me? I can bench two forty, and I run five miles every single day. Not to mention, I was on the NoCal crew team. And I won the Pebble Beach Yacht Club's catamaran race three years in a row."

"Oh," I said. No wonder the guy seemed to

have such a wicked build beneath his Polo. "So your death was accidental, then, I take it?"

"Damn straight it was accidental," Craig said, stabbing a finger into my mattress for emphasis. "That storm came out of nowhere. Flipped us right over before I had a chance to adjust the sail. Pinned me under."

"So . . ." I said hesitantly. "You drowned?"

Craig shook his head . . . not in answer to my question but out of frustration.

"It shouldn't have happened," he said, staring unseeingly at his shoes . . . deck shoes, the kind guys like him—boaters—wear without socks. "It wasn't supposed to have been me. I was on my high school swim team. I was first in the district one year in freestyle."

I still didn't get it.

"I'm sorry," I said. "I know it doesn't seem fair. But things will get better, I promise."

"Oh, really?" Craig looked up from his shoes, his hazel gaze seeming to pin me against the far wall. "How? How are things going to get better? In case you haven't noticed, I'm *dead*."

"She means things will get better for you when you've moved on," Jesse said, coming to my rescue. He seemed to have gotten over the pirate remark.

"Oh, things will get better, will they?" Craig let out a bitter laugh. "Like they have for you? Looks like you've been waiting to move on for a while, buddy. What's the holdup?"

Jesse didn't say anything. There wasn't really anything he *could* say. He didn't, of course, know why he hadn't yet passed from this world to the next. Neither did I. Whatever it was that was trapping Jesse in this time and place had a pretty solid hold on him, though: It had already kept him here for over a century and a half and showed every sign of hanging on—I selfishly hoped—for my lifetime anyway, if not all eternity.

And while Father Dom kept insisting that one of these days, Jesse was going to figure out what it was that was keeping him earthbound, and that I had better not get too attached to him since the day would come when I would never see him again, those well-meaning warnings had fallen on deaf ears. I was already attached. Big time.

And I wasn't working too hard on extricating myself from that attachment either.

"Jesse's situation is kind of unique," I said to Craig in what I hoped was a reassuring tone—both for his sake as well as Jesse's. "I'm sure yours is nowhere near as complicated."

"Damn straight," Craig said. "Because I'm not

even supposed to be here."

"Right," I said. "And I'm going to do my best to get you moving on to that next life of yours. . . ."

Craig frowned. It was the same frown he'd been wearing all through dinner, as he'd gazed at Jake's friend Neil.

"No," he said. "That's not what I meant. I mean I'm not supposed to be here. As in, I'm not supposed to be dead."

I nodded. I had heard this one before, countless times. No one wants to wake up and discover that he or she is no longer alive. No one.

"It's hard," I said. "I know it is. But eventually you'll adjust to the idea, I promise. And things will be better once we figure out what exactly is holding you back—"

"You don't get it," Craig said, shaking his dark head. "That's what I'm trying to tell you. What's holding me back is the fact that I'm not the one who's supposed to be dead."

I said hesitantly, "Well . . . that may be. But there's nothing I can do about that."

"What do you mean?" Craig rose to his feet and stood in my bedroom, looking furious. "What do you mean, there's nothing you can do about that? What am I doing here, then? I thought you said you could help me. I thought you said you were the mediator."

"I am," I said with a hasty glance at Jesse, who looked as taken aback as I felt. "But I don't dictate who lives or dies. That's not up to me. It's not part of my job."

Craig, his expression turning to one of disgust, said, "Well, thanks for nothing, then," and started stalking toward my bedroom door.

I wasn't about to stop him. I mean, I didn't really want anything more to do with him. He seemed like kind of a rude guy with a chip on his big swimmer's shoulders. If he didn't want my help, hey, not my problem.

It was Jesse who stopped him.

"You," he said, in a voice that was deep enough—and commanding enough—to cause Craig to stop in his tracks. "Apologize to her."

The guy in the doorway turned his head slowly to stare at Jesse.

"No freaking way," was what he had the lack of foresight to say.

A second later, he wasn't walking out—or even through—that door. No, he was pinned to it. Jesse was holding one of Craig's arms at what looked to be a fairly painful angle behind his back, and he was leaning heavily against him.

"Apologize," Jesse hissed, "to the young lady. She is trying to do you a kindness. You do not turn your back on someone who is trying to do you a kindness."

Whoa. For a guy who seems to want nothing to do with me, Jesse sure can be testy sometimes about how other people treat me.

"I'm sorry," Craig said in a voice that was muffled against the wood of the door. He sounded like he might be in pain. Just because you are dead, of course, does not mean you are immune to injury. Your soul remembers, even if your body is gone.

"That's better," Jesse said, releasing him.

Craig sagged against the door. Even though he was kind of a jerk and all, I felt sorry for the guy. I mean, he had had an even tougher day than I had, what with being dead and all.

"It's just," Craig said in a suffering tone as he reached up to rub the arm Jesse had nearly broken, "that it isn't fair, you know? It wasn't supposed to have been me. I was the one who should have lived. Not Neil."

I looked at him with some surprise. "Oh? Neil was with you on the boat?"

"Catamaran," Craig corrected me. "And yeah, of course he was."

"He was your sailing partner?"

Craig sent me a look of disgust, then, with a nervous glance at Jesse, quickly modified it to one of polite disdain.

"Of course not," he said. "Do you think we'd have tipped if Neil had had the slightest clue what he was doing? By rights, *he's* the one who should be dead. I don't know what Mom and Dad were thinking. *Take Neil out on the cat with you. You never take Neil out on the cat with you.* Well, I hope they're happy now. I took Neil out on the cat with me. And look where it got me. I'm dead. And my stupid brother is the one who lived."

chapter *six*

Well, at least now I knew why Neil had been sort of quiet all through dinner: He'd just lost his only brother.

"The guy couldn't swim to the other side of the pool," Craig insisted, "without having an asthma attack. How could he have clung to the side of a catamaran for seven hours, in ten-foot swells, before being rescued? How?"

I was at a loss to explain it as well. Much as I was at a loss as to how I was going to explain to Craig that it was his belief that his brother should be dead that was keeping his soul earthbound.

"Maybe," I suggested tentatively, "you got hit in the head."

"So what if I did?" Craig glared at me, letting me know my guess was right on target. "Freaking Neil—who couldn't do a chin-up to save his life— *he* managed to hold on. Me, the guy with all the swimming trophies? Yeah, I'm the one who drowned. There's no justice in the world. And that's why I'm here, and Neil's downstairs eating freaking fajitas."

Jesse looked solemn. "Is it your plan, then, to avenge your death by taking your brother's life, as you feel yours was taken?"

I winced. I could tell by Craig's expression that nothing of the kind had ever occurred to him. I was sorry Jesse had suggested it.

"No way, man," Craig said. Then, looking as if he was having second thoughts, he added, "Could I even do that? I mean, kill someone? If I wanted to?"

"No," I said, at the same time that Jesse said, "Yes, but you would be risking your immortal soul—"

Craig didn't listen to me, of course. Only to Jesse.

"Cool," he said, staring down at his own hands.

"No killing," I said loudly. "There will be no fratricide. Not on my watch."

Craig glanced up at me, looking surprised.

"I'm not gonna kill him," he said.

I shook my head. "Then what?" I asked. "What's holding you back? Was there . . . I don't know. Something left unsaid between the two of you? Do you want me to say it to him for you? Whatever it is?"

Craig looked at me like I was nuts.

"Neil?" he echoed. "Are you kidding me? I've got nothing to say to Neil. The guy's a tool. I mean, look at him, hanging around a guy like your brother."

While I myself do not hold my stepbrothers in very high esteem—with the exception of David, of course—that didn't mean I could sit idly by while someone maligned them to my face. At least, not Jake, who was, for the most part, fairly inoffensive.

"What's wrong with my brother?" I demanded a little hotly. "I mean, my stepbrother?"

"Well, nothing against him, really," Craig said. "But, you know . . . well. I mean, I know Neil's just a freshman and impressionable and all that, but I warned him, you can't get anywhere at NoCal unless you hang with the surfers."

I had, by that time, had about all I could take from Craig Jankow.

"Okay," I said, walking to my bedroom door.

"Well, it was great to meet you, Craig. You'll be hearing from me." He would, too. I'd know how to find him. All I'd have to do is look for Neil, and ten to one, I'd find Craig trailing along behind.

Craig looked eager. "You mean you're going to try to bring me back to life?"

"No," I said. "I mean, like, I'll determine why you are still here, and not where you're supposed to be."

"Right," Craig said. "Alive."

"I think she means in heaven," Jesse said. Jesse doesn't go much for the whole reincarnation thing the way I do. "Or hell."

Craig, who had taken to eyeing Jesse quite nervously since the whole incident by the door, looked alarmed.

"Oh," he said, his dark eyebrows raised. "*Oh*."

"Or your next life," I said with a meaningful look at Jesse. "We don't really know. Do we, Jesse?"

Jesse, who'd stood up because I'd stood up—and Jesse was nothing if not gentlemanly in front of ladies—said with obvious reluctance, "No. We don't."

Craig went to the door, then looked back at both of us.

"Well," he said. "See you around, I guess."

Then he glanced over at Jesse and said, "And, um, I'm sorry about that pirate remark. Really."

Jesse said gruffly, "That's all right."

Then Craig was gone.

And Jesse let loose.

"Susannah, that boy is trouble. You must turn him over to Father Dominic."

I sighed and sank down onto the place on the window seat that Jesse had just vacated. Spike, as was his custom when I approached and Jesse was anywhere in the near vicinity, hissed at me, to make it clear to whom he belonged . . . namely, not me, even though I am the one who pays for his food and litter.

"He'll be fine, Jesse," I said. "We'll keep an eye on him. He needs a little time is all. He just died, for crying out loud."

Jesse shook his head, his dark eyes flashing.

"He's going to try to kill his brother," he warned me.

"Well, yeah," I said. "Now that you put the idea in his head."

"You must call Father Dominic." Jesse strode over to the phone and picked it up. "Tell him he must meet with this boy, the brother, and warn him."

"Whoa," I said. "Slow down, Jesse. I can handle

this without having to drag Father Dom into it."

Jesse looked skeptical. The thing is, even when looking skeptical, Jesse is the hottest guy I have ever seen. I mean, he's not perfect-looking or anything—there's a scar through his right eyebrow, clean and white as a chalk mark, and he is, as I think I've observed before, somewhat fashion impaired.

But in every other way, the guy is Stud City, from the top of his close-cropped black hair to his swashbuckling—I mean, riding—boots, and the six feet or so of extremely uncadaverous-looking muscle in between.

Too bad his interest in me is apparently completely platonic. Maybe if I'd been a better kisser . . . But come on, it's not like I've had a lot of opportunity to practice. Guys—normal guys—don't exactly come flocking to my door. Not that I am a dog or anything. In fact, I think I look quite passable, when fully made up with my hair nicely blown out. It is just that it is a bit hard to have a social life when you are constantly being solicited by the dead.

"I think you should call him," Jesse said, thrusting the phone at me again. "I am telling you, *querida*. There is more to this Craig than meets the eye."

I blinked, but not because of what Jesse had said about Craig. No, it was because of what he'd called me. *Querida*. He hadn't called me that, not once, since that day we'd kissed. I had, in fact, missed hearing the word from his lips so much that I had actually gotten curious about what it meant and looked it up in Brad's Spanish dictionary.

"Dearest one." That is what *querida* meant. "Dearest one," or "sweetheart."

Which isn't exactly what you call someone for whom you feel mere friendship.

I hoped.

I didn't let on, however, that I knew what the word meant, any more than I let on that I'd noticed he'd allowed it to slip out.

"You're overreacting, Jesse," I said. "Craig's not going to do anything to his brother. He loves the guy. He just doesn't seem to have remembered that yet. And, besides, even if he didn't—even if he did have homicidal intentions toward Neil— what makes you think all of a sudden that I can't handle it? I mean, come on, Jesse. It's not like I'm unaccustomed to bloodthirsty ghosts."

Jesse put the phone down so hard that I thought he'd cracked the plastic cradle.

"That was before," he said shortly.

I stared at him. It had grown dark outside, and the only light on in my room was the little one on my dressing table. In its golden glow, Jesse looked even more otherwordly than usual.

"Before what?" I demanded.

Except that I knew. I knew.

"Before *he* came," Jesse said, with a certain amount of bitter emphasis on the pronoun. "And don't try to deny it, Susannah. You have not slept a full night since. I have seen you tossing and turning. You cry out in your sleep sometimes."

I didn't have to ask who *he* was. I knew. We both knew.

"That's nothing," I said, even though of course it wasn't. It was something. It was definitely something. Just not what Jesse apparently thought it was. "I mean, I'm not saying I wasn't scared when you and I thought we were trapped in that . . . place. And, yeah, I have nightmares about it, sometimes. But I'll get over it, Jesse. I'm getting over it."

"You aren't invulnerable, Susannah," Jesse said with a frown. "However much you might think differently."

I was more than a little surprised that he'd noticed. In fact, I'd begun to wonder if perhaps it was because I didn't act vulnerable—or, okay, feminine—enough that he'd only grabbed and kissed me that once, and never tried to do it again.

Except of course as soon as he accused me of being vulnerable, I had to go and deny it was true.

"I'm fine," I insisted. No point in mentioning to him that, in fact, I was far from fine . . . that the mere sight of Paul Slater had nearly caused me to have a heart attack. "I told you. I'm over it, Jesse. And even if I wasn't, it's not like it's going to keep me from helping Craig. Or Neil, really."

But it was like he wasn't even listening.

"Let Father Dominic take this one," Jesse said. He nodded toward the door through which Craig had just walked—literally. "You aren't ready yet. It's too soon."

Now I wished I had told him about Paul . . . told him nonchalantly, as if it were nothing, to prove to him that's that what it was to me . . . nothing.

Except of course it wasn't. And it never would be.

"Your solicitude," I said sarcastically in order to hide my discomfort over the whole thing—the fact that I was lying to him, not just about Paul but about myself as well—"is appreciated but misplaced. I can handle Craig Jankow, Jesse."

He frowned again. But this time, I could see, he really was annoyed. Were we ever to actually date, I knew it would take a lot of *Oprah* viewing before Jesse learned to get over his nineteenth-century machismo.

"I will go," he said threateningly, his dark eyes looking black as onyx in the light from my dressing table, "and tell Father Dominic myself."

"Fine," I said. "Be my guest."

Which wasn't what I'd wanted to say, of course. What I'd wanted to say was, *Why? Why can't we be together, Jesse? I know you want to. Don't even bother denying it. I felt it when you kissed me. I may not have a lot of experience in that department, but I know I'm not wrong about that. You like me, at least a little. So what's the deal? Why have you been giving me the cold shoulder ever since? WHY?*

Whatever the reason might have been, Jesse wasn't revealing it just then. Instead, he set his jaw, and went, "Fine, I will."

"Go ahead," I shot back.

A second later, he was gone. *Poof*, just like that.

Well, who needed him, anyway?

All right. I did. I admit it.

But I tried resolutely to put him out of my head. I concentrated instead on my trig homework.

I was still concentrating on it when fourth period—computer lab, for me—rolled around the next day. I am telling you, there is nothing more devastating to a girl's ability to study than a handsome ghost who thinks he knows everything.

I was, of course, supposed to be working on a five-hundred-word essay on the Civil War, which had been punitively assigned to the entire eleventh grade by our advisor, Mr. Walden, who had not appreciated the behavior of a few of us during that morning's nominations for student government positions.

In particular, Mr. Walden had not appreciated my behavior when, after Kelly's nomination of Paul for vice president had been seconded and passed, CeeCee had raised her hand and nominated me for vice president as well.

"Ow," CeeCee had cried, when I'd kicked her, hard, beneath her desk. "What is *wrong* with you?"

"I don't want to be vice president," I'd hissed at her. "Put your arm down."

This had resulted in a good deal of snickering, which had not died down until Mr. Walden, never the world's most patient instructor, threw a piece of chalk at the classroom door and told us we'd all better brush up on our American history—five hundred words on the Battle of Gettysburg, to be exact.

But my objection came too late. CeeCee's nomination of me was seconded by Adam, and passed a second later, despite my protests. I was now running for vice president of the junior class—CeeCee was my campaign manager, Adam, whose grandfather had left him a healthy trust fund, the main financial contributor to my bid for election—against the new guy, Paul Slater, whose aw-shucks manner and stunning good looks had already won him almost every female vote in the class.

Not that I cared. I didn't want to be VP anyway. I had enough on my hands, what with the mediator thing and trigonometry and my dead would-be boyfriend. I did not need to have to worry about political mudslinging on top of all that.

It hadn't been a good morning. The nominations had been bad enough; Mr. Walden's essay put a nice cap on it.

And then, of course, there was Paul. He'd winked suggestively to me in homeroom, as if to say hello.

As if all of that hadn't been enough, I had foolishly chosen to wear a brand-new pair of Jimmy Choo mules to school, purchased at a fraction of their normal retail cost at an outlet over the summer. They were gorgeous, and they went perfectly with the Calvin Klein black denim skirt I had paired with a hot pink scoop-neck top.

But of course they were killing me. I already had raw, painful blisters around the bases of all my toes, and the Band-Aids the nurse had given me to cover them so that I could at least hobble between classes were not exactly doing the job. My feet felt like they were about to fall off. If I'd known where Jimmy Choo lived, I would have hobbled right up to his front door and popped him one in the eye.

So I was sitting there in the computer lab, my mules kicked off and my toes throbbing painfully, working on my trig homework when I should have been working on my essay, when a voice I had come to know as well as my own startled me by saying, close to my ear, "Miss me, Suze?"

chapter *seven*

"Leave me alone," I said more calmly than I felt.

"Aw, come on, Simon," Paul said, reaching for a nearby chair, swinging it around, and then straddling it. "Admit it. You don't hate me half as much as you pretend to."

"I wouldn't bet on it," I said. I tapped my pencil against my notebook with what I hoped he would take to be irritation but which was, in fact, nervous tension. "Listen, Paul, I have a lot of work to do—"

He plucked the notebook out from beneath my hands. "Who's Craig Jankow?"

Startled, I realized I had doodled the name in the margin of my worksheet.

"Nobody," I said.

"Oh, that's good," Paul said. "I thought maybe he'd gone and replaced me in your affections. Does Jesse know? About this Craig guy, I mean?"

I glared at him, hoping he'd mistake my fear for anger and go away. He didn't seem to be getting the message, though. I hoped he couldn't see how rapidly my pulse was beating in my throat . . . or that if he did, he didn't mistake it for something it was not. Paul was not unaware of his good looks, unfortunately. He had on black jeans that fit him in all the right places and an olive-green short-sleeved Polo shirt. It brought out the deepness of his golf-and-tennis tan. I could see the other girls in the computer lab—Debbie Mancuso, for one—peeking at Paul speculatively, then looking quickly back at their computer monitors, trying to act as if they hadn't been trying to scope him out a minute before.

They were probably seething with jealousy that he was talking to me, of all people—the only girl in their class who didn't let Kelly Prescott tell her what to do and who didn't consider Brad Ackerman a hottie.

Little did they know how much I would have appreciated it if Paul Slater hadn't chosen to grace me with his company.

"Craig," I whispered, just in case anyone was listening, "happens to be dead."

"So?" Paul grinned at me. "I thought that was how you liked 'em."

"You"—I tried to snatch the notebook back from him, but he held it out of my reach—"are insufferable."

He looked meditative as he studied the problems on my worksheet. "There's something to be said for having a dead boyfriend, I suppose," he mused. "I mean, you don't have to worry about introducing him to your parents, since they can't see him, anyway. . . ."

"Craig's not my boyfriend," I hissed at him, angry at finding myself in a situation where I was explaining anything to Paul Slater. "I'm trying to help him. He showed up at my house yesterday—"

"Oh, God." Paul rolled his expressive blue eyes. "Not another one of those charity cases you and the good father are always taking on."

I said with some indignation, "Helping lost souls find their way is my job, after all."

"Who says?" Paul wanted to know.

I blinked at him. "Well—it just—it just *is*," I stammered. "I mean, what else am I supposed to do?"

Paul plucked a pencil from a nearby desk and

began swiftly and neatly to solve the problems on my worksheet. "I wonder. It doesn't seem fair to me that we were just handed this mediator thing at birth without so much as a contract or list of employee benefits. I mean, I never signed up for this mediator thing. Did you?"

"Of course not," I said, as if this was not something about which I complained, in almost those exact words, every time I saw Father Dominic.

"And how do you know what your job responsibilities even consist of?" Paul asked. "Yeah, you think you're supposed to help the dead move on to their final destination, because once you do, they stop bugging you, and you can get on with your life again. But I've got a question for you. Who told you it was up to you? Who told you how it was done, even?"

I blinked at him. No one had told me that, actually. Well, my dad had, sort of. And later, a certain psychic my best friend, Gina, had taken me to back home. And then Father Dom, of course . . .

"Right," Paul said, observing from my expression apparently that I didn't have a real straightforward answer for him. "Nobody told you. But what if I said I knew? What if I told you I'd found something—something that dated back to the first days of actual written communication—that exactly described mediators, though that wasn't what we were called back then, and their real purpose, not to mention techniques?"

I continued to blink at him. He sounded so . . . well, convincing. And he certainly looked sincere.

"If you really had something like that," I said hesitantly, "I guess I'd say . . . show me."

"Fine," Paul said, looking pleased. "Come over to my place after school today, and I will."

I was up and out of my chair so fast, I practically tipped it over.

"No," I said, gathering up my books and clutching them in front of my wildly beating heart as if both to hide and protect it. "*No way.*"

Paul regarded me from where he sat, not seeming too surprised by my reaction.

"Hmmm," he said. "I thought as much. You want to know but not enough to risk your reputation."

"It isn't my reputation I'm worried about," I informed him, managing to make my tone more acid than shaken. "It's my life. You tried to kill me once, remember?"

I said these words a little too loudly and noticed several people glance at me curiously over the tops of the computer monitors.

Paul, however, just looked bored.

"Not that again," he said. "Listen, Suze, I told you. . . . Well, I guess it doesn't matter what I told you. You're going to believe what you want to believe. But, seriously, you could have gotten out of there any time you wanted to."

"But Jesse couldn't have," I hissed at him. "Could he? Thanks to you."

"Well," Paul said with an uncomfortable shrug. "No. Not Jesse. But, really, Suze, don't you think you're overreacting? I mean, what's the big deal? The guy's already dead—"

"You," I said, my trembling voice giving the statement somewhat iffy conviction, "are a pig."

Then I started to stride away. I say started to because I didn't get very far before Paul's calm voice stopped me.

"Uh, Suze," Paul said. "Aren't you forgetting something?"

I turned my head to glare at him. "Oh, you mean, did I forget to tell you not to speak to me again? Yes."

"No," Paul said with a wry smile. "Aren't those your shoes under there?" He pointed down at my Jimmy Choos, without which I'd been about to stalk from the room. Like Sister Ernestine wouldn't have had too big a coronary if she'd caught me wandering around school in my bare feet.

"Oh," I said, mad that my dramatic exit had been spoiled. "Yeah." I went back to my desk so I could jam my feet into my mules.

"Before you go, Cinderella," Paul said, still smiling, "you might also want to take this." He held out my trig homework. I could tell with a single glance that he'd finished it, neatly and, I could only assume, correctly.

"Thanks," I said, taking the notebook from him, feeling more and more sheepish with every passing second. I mean, why, exactly, was I always flying off the handle with this guy? Yeah, he'd tried to kill me—and Jesse—once. At least, I thought he had. But he kept saying I was wrong. What if I *was* wrong? What if Paul wasn't the monster I'd always thought him? What if he was . . .

What if he was just like me?

"About this Craig guy," Paul added.

"Paul." I sank down into the chair beside him. I had felt the gaze of Mrs. Tarentino, the teacher assigned to supervise the computer lab, boring into me. Popping in and out of your chair in the lab is not smiled upon, unless you are going back and forth from the printer.

But that wasn't the only reason I sat down

again. I'll admit that. I was curious, too. Curious over what he'd say next. And that curiosity was almost stronger than my fear.

"Seriously," I said. "Thanks. But I do not need your help."

"I think you do," Paul said. "What's this Craig guy want, anyway?"

"He wants what all ghosts want," I said tiredly. "To be alive again."

"Well, of course," Paul said. "I mean, what's he want besides that?"

"I don't know yet," I said with a shrug. "He's got this thing with his little brother . . . thinks he should have been the one to die, not him. Jesse thinks—" I stopped talking, suddenly aware that Jesse was the last person I wanted to bring up in front of Paul.

Paul looked only politely interested, however. "Jesse thinks what?"

It was, I saw, too late to keep Jesse out of it. I sighed and said, "Jesse thinks Craig's going to try to kill his brother. You know. Out of revenge."

"Which, will, of course," Paul said, not looking in the least surprised, "get him exactly nowhere. When will they ever learn? Now, if he wanted to *be* his brother, that would be a different story."

"*Be* his brother?" I looked at him curiously.

"What do you mean?"

"You know," Paul said with a shrug. "Soul transference. Take over his brother's body."

This was a little too much for a Tuesday morning. I mean, I had already had a pretty crummy night's sleep thanks to this guy. Then, to hear something like this come out of his mouth . . . well, let's just say I was not at my sharpest, so what happened next can hardly be described as my fault.

"*Take over his brother's body?*" I echoed. I had lowered my books until they rested in my lap. Now I reached out and gripped the arms of my computer chair, my nails sinking into the cheap foam-padded armrests. "What are you talking about?"

One of Paul's dark eyebrows hiked up. "Doesn't sound familiar, eh? What *has* the good father been teaching you, I wonder? Not much, from the sound of things."

"What are you talking about?" I demanded. "How can someone take over someone else's body?"

"I told you," Paul said, leaning back in his chair and folding his hands behind his head, "that there was a lot you didn't know about being a mediator. And a lot more that I could teach you, if you'd just give me the chance."

I stared at him. I really had no idea what he was talking about with this body-swapping thing. It sounded like something from the Sci-Fi Channel. And I wasn't sure if Paul was just feeding me a line, something, anything, to get me to do what he wanted.

But what if he wasn't? What if there was seriously a way to—

I wanted to know. My God, I wanted to know more than I had ever wanted anything in my life.

"All right," I said, feeling the sweat that had broken out beneath my palms, making the chair's armrests slick with moisture. But I didn't care. My heart was in my throat, and still I didn't care. "All right. I'll come over to your place after school. But only if you'll tell me about . . . about that."

Something flashed through Paul's blue eyes. Just a gleam, and I saw it only for a moment before it was gone again. It was something animal-like, almost feral. I couldn't say just what, exactly, it had been.

All I knew was that the next minute, Paul was smiling at me—smiling, not grinning.

"Fine," he said. "I'll pick you up by the main gate at three. Be there on time, or I'll leave without you."

chapter *eight*

I wasn't, of course, going to meet him. I mean, despite ample evidence to the contrary, I am not stupid. I have, in the past, met various people at various appointed times and found myself, hours later, either tied to a chair, thrust into a parallel dimension, forced to don one-piece swimsuits, or being otherwise cruelly mistreated. I was not going to meet Paul Slater after school. I was so not.

And then I did anyway.

Well, what else was I supposed to do? The lure was just too great. I mean, actual documented evidence about mediators? Something about people being able to take over other people's bodies?

All the nightmares about long, fog-enshrouded hallways in the world were not going to keep me from finding out the truth at last about what I was and what I could do. I had spent too many years wondering just that to allow an opportunity like this to slip from my fingers. I had never, unlike Father Dominic, been able merely to accept the cards I'd been dealt. . . . I wanted to know why they'd been dealt to me and how. I *had* to know.

And if, in order to find out, I had to spend time with someone who regularly haunted my sleep, so be it. It was worth the sacrifice.

Or I hoped it would be, anyway.

Adam and CeeCee weren't too happy about it, of course. As the last class of the day let out, they met me in the hallway—I was visibly limping, thanks to my shoes, but CeeCee didn't notice. She was too busy consulting the list she'd drawn up in bio.

"All right," she said. "We've got to head on over to Safeway for markers, glitter, glue, and poster board. Adam, does your mom still have those dowels in the garage from when she went on that Amish chair-making kick? Because we could use them for the Vote for Suze placards."

"Uh," I said, hobbling along beside them. "You guys."

"Suze, can we take all the stuff over to your place to assemble it? I'd say we could take it to my place, but you know my sisters. They'll probably roller-skate over it or whatever."

"Guys," I said. "Look. I appreciate this and all. I really do. But I can't come with you. I've already got plans."

Adam and CeeCee exchanged glances.

"Oh?" CeeCee said. "Meeting the mysterious Jesse, are we?"

"Uh," I said. "Not exactly—"

At that moment, Paul came past us in the hall. He said to me, noticing my limp, "Let me just pull the car around to the side door. That way you won't have to walk to the gate," and breezed on by.

Adam gave me a scandalized look. "Fraternizing with the enemy!" he cried. "For shame, wench!"

CeeCee looked equally stunned. "You're going out with *him*?" She shook her head so that her stick-straight white-blond hair shimmered. "What about Jesse?"

"I'm not going out with him," I said uncomfortably. "We're just . . . working on a project together."

"What project?" CeeCee's eyes, behind the lenses of her glasses, narrowed. "For what class?"

"It's . . ." I shifted my weight from one foot to the other, hoping to find some relief from my cruel shoes, all to no avail. "It's not for school, really. It's more for . . . for . . . church."

Even as the word came out of my mouth, I knew I'd made a mistake. CeeCee wouldn't mind being left alone with Adam—in fact, she'd probably love it—but she wasn't about to let me off the hook without a good reason.

"*Church?*" CeeCee looked mad. "You're Jewish, Suze, in case I need to remind you."

"Well, not technically, really," I said. "I mean, my dad was, but my mom isn't—" A car horn sounded just beyond the ornately scrolled gate we were standing behind. "Oops, that's Paul. Gotta go, sorry."

Then, moving pretty quickly for a girl who felt shooting stabs of pain go up her legs with every step, I hightailed it out to Paul's convertible and slid into the passenger seat with a sigh of relief at being in a seated position once more and a feeling that, at last, I was going to find out a thing or two about who—or what—I really was. . . .

But I had an equally strong feeling that I wasn't going to like what I found out. In fact, a part of me was wondering whether or not I was making the worst mistake of my life.

It didn't help matters much that Paul, with his dark sunglasses and easy smile, looked like a movie star. Really, how could I have had so many nightmares about this guy who was so clearly any normal girl's dream date? I didn't miss the envious glances that were being shot in my direction from around the parking lot.

"Did I happen to mention," Paul asked, as I fastened my seat belt, "that I think those shoes are flickin'?"

I swallowed. I didn't even know what *flicking* meant. I could only assume from his tone that it meant something good.

Did I really want to do this? Was it worth it?

The answer came from deep within . . . so deep, I realized that I had known it all along: Yes. Oh, yes.

"Just drive," I said, my voice coming out huskier than usual, because I was trying not to let my nervousness show.

And so he did.

The house he drove me to was an impressive two-storied structure built into the side of a cliff right off Carmel Beach. It was made almost entirely of glass in order to take advantage of its ocean and sunset views.

Paul seemed to notice that I was impressed,

since he said, "It's my grandfather's place. He wanted a little place on the beach to retire to."

"Right," I said, swallowing hard. Grandpa Slater's "little" place on the beach had to have cost a cool five million or so. "And he doesn't mind having a roommate all of a sudden?"

"Are you kidding?" Paul smirked as he parked his car in one of the spaces of the house's four-car garage. "He barely knows I'm here. The guy's gorked out on his meds most of the time."

"Paul," I said uncomfortably.

"What?" Paul blinked at me from behind his Ray-Bans. "I'm just stating a fact. Pops is pretty much bedridden and should be in an assisted living facility, but he put up this huge fuss when we tried to move him to one. So when I suggested I move in to kind of keep an eye on things, my dad agreed. It's a win-win situation. Pops gets to live at home—with health-care attendants to look after him, of course—and I get to attend my dream school, the Mission Academy."

I felt my face heat up, but I tried to keep my tone light.

"Oh, so going to Catholic school is your dream?" I asked sarcastically.

"It is if you're there," Paul said, just as lightly . . . but not quite as sarcastically.

My face promptly turned red as a cherry-dipped cone. Keeping it averted so that Paul wouldn't notice, I said primly, "I don't think this such a good idea, after all."

"Relax, Simon," Paul drawled. "Pop's day attendant is here, in case you're, you know, suffering from any feminine misgivings about being alone in the house with me."

I followed the direction Paul was pointing. At the end of the steep circular drive sat a rusted-out Toyota Celica. I didn't say anything, but mostly only because I was kind of amazed at how easily Paul seemed to have read my mind. I had been sitting there, suffering from second thoughts about the whole thing. I had never exactly raised the issue with my parents, but I was pretty sure I wasn't allowed to go to guys' houses when their parents weren't home.

On the other hand, if I didn't in this case, I would never find out what I needed—and I was convinced by now that this was something I actually really did need—to know.

Paul slid out from behind the wheel, then walked around to my side of the car and opened the door for me.

"Coming, Suze?" he asked, when I didn't move to undo my seat belt.

"Uh," I said, looking nervously up at the big glass house. It looked disturbingly empty, despite the Toyota.

Paul seemed to read my mind again.

"Would you get off it, Suze?" he said, rolling his eyes. "Your virtue's in no danger from me. I swear I'll keep my hands to myself. This is business. There'll be plenty of time for fun later."

I tried to smile coolly, so he wouldn't suspect that I am not accustomed to people—okay, guys—saying this sort of thing to me every day. But the truth is, of course I'm not. And it bugged me the way it made me feel when Paul did it. I mean, I did not even like this guy, but every time he said something like that—suggested that he thought I was, I don't know, special—it sent this little shiver down my spine . . . and not in a bad way.

That was the thing. *It wasn't in a bad way.* What was *that* all about? I mean, I don't even like Paul. I am fully in love with somebody else. And, yeah, Jesse is presently showing no signs of actually returning my feelings, but it's not like because of that I am suddenly going to start going out with Paul Slater . . . no matter how good he might look in his Ray-Bans.

I got out of the car.

"Wise decision," Paul commented, closing the car door behind me.

There was a sort of finality in the sound of that door being slammed shut. I tried not to think about what I might be letting myself in for as I followed Paul up the cement steps to the wide glass front door to his grandfather's house, barefoot, my Jimmy Choos in one hand and my book bag in the other.

Inside the Slaters' house, it was cool and quiet . . . so quiet, you couldn't even hear the pounding surf of the ocean not a hundred feet below it. Whoever had decorated the place had taste that ran toward the modern, so everything looked sleek and new and uncomfortable. The house, I imagined, must have been freezing in the morning when the fog rolled in, since everything in it was made of glass or metal. Paul led me up a twisting steel staircase from the front door to the high-tech kitchen, where all the appliances gleamed aggressively.

"Cocktail?" he asked me, opening a glass door to a liquor cabinet.

"Very funny," I said. "Just water, please. Where's your grandfather?"

"Down the hall," Paul said, as he pulled two bottles of designer water from the enormous

Sub-Zero fridge. He must have noticed my nervous glance over my shoulder, since he added, "Go take a look for yourself if you don't believe me."

I went to take a look for myself. It wasn't that I didn't trust him . . . well, okay, it was. Though it would have been pretty bold of him to lie about something I could so easily check. And what was I going to do if it turned out his grandfather wasn't there? I mean, no way was I leaving before I'd found out what I'd come to learn.

Fortunately, it appeared I wouldn't have to. Hearing some faint sounds, I followed them down a long glass hallway, until I came to a room in which a wide-screen television was on. In front of the television sat a very old man in a very high-tech wheelchair. Beside the wheelchair, in a very uncomfortable-looking modern chair, sat a youngish guy in a blue nurse's uniform, reading a magazine. He looked up when I appeared in the doorway and smiled.

"Hey," he said.

"Hey," I said back, and came tentatively into the room. It was a nice room, with one of the better views in the house, I imagined. It had been furnished with a hospital bed, complete with an IV bag and adjustable frame and metal bookshelves on which rested frame after frame of photographs.

Black-and-white photographs mostly, judging by their outfits, of people from the forties.

"Um," I said to the old man in the wheelchair. "Hi, Mr. Slater. I'm Susannah Simon."

The old man didn't say anything. He didn't even take his gaze from the game show that was on in front of him. He was mostly bald and pretty much covered in liver spots, and he was drooling a little. The nurse noticed this and leaned over with a handkerchief to wipe the old man's mouth.

"There you go, Mr. Slater," the nurse said. "The nice young lady said hello. Aren't you going to say hello back?"

But Mr. Slater didn't say anything. Instead, Paul, who'd come into the room behind me, went, "How's it going, Pops? Had another riveting day in front of the old boob tube?"

Mr. Slater did not acknowledge Paul, either. The nurse said, "We had a good day, didn't we, Mr. Slater? Took a nice walk in the backyard around the pool and picked a few lemons."

"That's great," Paul said with forced enthusiasm. Then he took my hand and started to drag me from the room. I will admit he didn't have to drag hard. I was pretty creeped out, and went willingly enough. Which is saying a lot, considering how I felt about Paul and everything. I mean, that there was someone who creeped me out more than he did.

"Bye, Mr. Slater," I said, not expecting a response . . . which was a good thing, since I got none.

Out in the hallway, I asked quietly, "What's wrong with him? Alzheimer's?"

"Naw," Paul said, handing me one of the dark-blue bottles of water. "They don't know, exactly. He's lucid enough, when he wants to be."

"Really?" I had a hard time believing it. Lucid people can usually maintain some control over their own saliva. "Maybe he's just . . . you know. Old."

"Yeah," Paul said with another of his trade-mark bitter laughs. "That's probably it, all right." Then, without elaborating further, he threw open a door on his right and said, "This is it. What I wanted to show you."

I followed him into what was, clearly, his bed-room. It was about five times as big as my own room—and Paul's bed was about five times big-ger than mine. Like the rest of the house, every-thing was very streamlined and modern, with a lot of metal and glass. There was even a glass desk—or Plexiglas, probably—on which rested a brand-new, top-of-the-line laptop. There was none of the kind of personal stuff lying around Paul's room that always seemed to be scattered around mine—like magazines or dirty socks or nail polish or half-eaten boxes of Girl Scout cookies. There was nothing personal in Paul's room at all. It was like a very high-tech, very cold hotel room.

"It's here," Paul said, sitting down on the edge of his boat-sized bed.

"Yeah," I said, more spooked than ever now . . . and not just because Paul was patting the empty space on the mattress beside him. No, it was also the fact that the only color in the room, besides what Paul and I were wearing, was what I could see out the enormous plate glass windows: the blue, blue sky and below it, the darker blue sea. "Sure it is."

"I'm serious," Paul said, and he quit patting the mattress like he wanted me to sit beside him. Instead, he reached beneath the bed and pulled out a clear plastic box, like the kind you store wool sweaters in over the summer.

Placing the box beside him on the bed, Paul pulled off the lid. Inside were what looked to be a number of newspaper and magazine articles, each one carefully clipped from its original source.

"Check these out," Paul said, carefully unfolding a particularly ancient newspaper article and spreading it out across the slate-gray bedspread so that I could see it. It came from the London *Times*, and was dated June 18, 1952. There was a photograph of a man standing before what looked like the hieroglyphic-covered wall of an Egyptian tomb. The headline above the photo and article ran, ARCHAEOLOGIST'S THEORY SCOFFED AT BY SKEPTICS.

"Dr. Oliver Slaski—that's this guy here in the photo—worked for years to translate the text on the wall of King Tut's tomb," Paul explained. "He came to the conclusion that in ancient Egypt there was actually a small group of shamans who had the ability to travel in and out of the realm of the dead without, in fact, dying themselves. These shamans were called, as near as Dr. Slaski could translate, shifters. They could shift from this plane of being to the next, and were hired as spirit guides for the deceased by the deceased's family, in order to ensure their loved one's ending up where he was supposed to instead of aimlessly wandering the planet."

I had sunk down onto the bed as Paul had been speaking so that I could get a better look at the picture he was indicating. I had been hesitant to do so before—I didn't really want to get near Paul at all, especially considering the whole bed thing.

Now, however, I hardly noticed how close we were sitting together. I leaned forward to stare at the picture until my hair brushed against the cracked and yellowed paper.

"Shifters," I said, through lips that had gone strangely cold, as if I had put Carmex on them. Only I hadn't. "What he meant was mediators."

"I don't think so," Paul said.

"No," I said. I was feeling sort of breathless. Well, you would, too, if your whole life you had wondered why you were so different from everyone you knew and then all of a sudden, one day you found out. Or at least got hold of a very important clue.

"That is exactly what it means, Paul," I exclaimed. "The ninth card in the tarot deck—the one called the Hermit—features an old man holding a lantern, just like this guy is doing," I said, indicating the guy in the hieroglyphic. "It always comes up when my cards are read. And the Hermit is a spirit guide, someone who is supposed to lead the dead to their final destination. And okay, the guy in the hieroglyphic isn't old, but they are both doing the same thing. . . . He has to mean mediators, Paul," I said, my heart thudding hard against my ribs. This was big. Really big. The fact that there was actual documented proof of the existence of people like me . . . I had never hoped to see such a thing. I couldn't wait to tell Father Dominic. "He *has* to!"

"But that's not all they were, Suze," Paul said, reaching back into the acrylic box and bringing out a sheaf of papers, also brown with age. "According to Slaski, who wrote this thesis about it, back in ancient Egypt there were your run-of-the-mill mediums, or, if you prefer, mediators. But then there were also shifters. And that," Paul said, looking at me very intently from across the bed, and not very far across the bed, either, as we were leaning only about a foot apart, the pages of Dr. Slaski's thesis between us, "is what you and I are, Suze. Shifters."

Again, I felt the chill. It raced up and down my spine, made the hairs on my arms stand up. I don't know what it was—the word *shifters,* or the way Paul said it. But it had an effect on me . . . quite an effect on me. Like sticking my finger in a light socket.

I shook my head. "No," I said in a panicky voice. "Not me. I'm just a mediator. I mean, if I were a shifter, I wouldn't have had to exorcise myself that time—"

"You didn't have to," Paul interrupted, his voice, compared to the high-pitched squeak mine had become, deep and calm. "You could have gotten yourself there—and back—on your own, just by visualizing the place. You could do it right now, if you wanted to."

I blinked at him. Paul's eyes, I noticed, above the crinkled pages of Dr. Slaski's thesis, were very bright. They almost seemed to gleam like cat's eyes. I could not tell if he was telling the truth or simply trying to mess with my head. Knowing Paul, either would not have surprised me. He seemed to get pleasure out of blurting things out, then seeing how people—all right, me—reacted.

"No way," was how I responded to his suggestion that I was anything but what I'd always thought I was. Even though the whole reason I was even in his bedroom was because deep down, I knew I was not.

"Try it," Paul urged. "Picture it in your head. You know what the place looks like now."

Did I ever. Thanks to him, I'd been trapped there for the longest fifteen minutes of my life. I was still trapped there, every single night, in my dreams. Even now, I could hear my heartbeat drumming in my ears as I tore down that long dark corridor, fog swirling and then parting around my legs. Did Paul really think that, even for a second, I ever wanted to visit that place again?

"No," I said. "No, thanks—"

Paul's smile turned wry.

"Don't tell me Suze Simon is actually afraid of something." His eyes seemed to glow more brightly than ever. "You always act as if you were immune to fear the way some people are immune to chicken pox."

"I'm not afraid." I lied with feigned indignation. "I just don't feel like—what is it called again? Oh, yeah, shifting—right now. Maybe later. Right now I want to ask you about that other thing you mentioned. The thing where somebody can take over somebody else's body. Soul transference."

Paul's smile broadened. "I thought that one might get your attention."

I knew what he was referring to—or thought I did, anyway. I could feel my face heating up. I ignored my burning cheeks, however, and said, with what I hoped sounded like cool indifference, "It sounds interesting, is all. Is it really possible?" I plucked at the crumpled pages of the thesis that lay between us. "Does Dr. Slaski mention it at all?"

"Maybe," Paul said, laying a hand down over

the typewritten sheets so that I could not lift them.

"Paul," I said, tugging on the sheets. "I'm just curious. I mean, have you ever done it? Does it actually work? Could Craig really take over his brother's body?"

But Paul wouldn't let go of Dr. Slaski's papers.

"It's not because of Craig that you're asking, though, is it?" His blue-eyed gaze bore into me. There wasn't the slightest hint of a smile on his face anymore. "Suze, when are you going to get it?"

That was when I finally noticed how close his face was to mine. Just inches away, really. I started instinctively to pull away, but the fingers that had been holding down Dr. Slaski's papers suddenly lifted and seized my wrist. I looked down at Paul's hand. His tanned skin was very dark against mine.

"Jesse's dead," Paul said. "But that doesn't mean you have to act like you are, too."

"I don't," I protested. "I—"

But I didn't get to finish my little speech, because right in the middle of it, Paul leaned over and kissed me.

chapter *nine*

I won't lie to you. It was a good kiss. I felt it all the way down to my poor, blistered toes.

Which is not to say I kissed him back. I most definitely did not. . . .

Well, okay. Not that much, anyway.

It was just that, you know, Paul was such a *good* kisser. And I hadn't been kissed in a very long time. It felt nice to know that *someone*, at least, wanted me. Even if that someone happened to be a person I despised. Or at least someone I was pretty sure I despised.

The truth was, it was sort of hard to remember whether or not I despised Paul. Not while he was kissing me so thoroughly. I mean, it isn't every day—unfortunately—that hot guys go around grabbing and kissing me. In fact, it had really only happened a handful of times before.

And when Paul Slater did it . . . well, let's just say that the last thing I was expecting was to *like* it. I mean, this was the same guy who'd tried to kill me not so long ago. . . .

Only now he was saying that this wasn't true, that I'd never been in any danger.

Except that I knew this was a lie. I was in plenty of danger—not of being killed but of completely losing my head for a guy who was bad for me in every way and even worse for the guy I loved. Because that's exactly how Paul Slater's kiss made me feel. Like I'd do anything—*anything*—to be kissed by him some more.

Which was just plain wrong. Because I wasn't in love with Paul Slater. Granted, the guy I was in love with was

A. dead, and

B. apparently not real interested in pursuing a romantic relationship with me.

But that didn't mean it was permissible for me to fling myself at the very next hottie who happened to come along. I mean, a girl has to have some principles . . . .

Such as saving herself for the guy she really

likes, even if he happens to be too stupid to realize they are perfect for each other.

So even though Paul's kiss made me feel like throwing my free arm around his neck and kissing him back—which I may or may not, in the heat of the moment, actually have done—it would have been wrong, wrong, WRONG.

So I tried to pull away.

Only let me tell you, that grip he had on my wrist? It was like iron. *Iron.*

And even worse, thanks to my having encouraged him by kissing him back a little, half his body ended up over mine, pressing me back onto the bed and probably wrinkling Dr. Slaski's thesis pretty badly. I know it wasn't doing any good for my Calvin Klein jean skirt.

So then I had like a hundred and eighty pounds or something of seventeen-year-old guy on top of me, which is not, you know, any picnic, when it isn't the guy you *want* to be on top of you. Or even if it is, but you are doing your best to stay true to someone else . . . someone who, to the best of your knowledge, doesn't even want you. But whatever.

I managed to wrestle my lips away from Paul's long enough to say in a sort of strangled voice since he was crushing my lungs, "Get off me."

"Come on, Suze," he said in a tone that, I'm sorry to say, sounded as if it were heavy. With passion. Or something, anyway. I'm even more sorry to say that the sound of it thrilled along every nerve in my body. I mean, that passion was for *me*. Me, Suze Simon, about whom no guy had ever felt all that passionate. At least so far as I knew. "Don't tell me you haven't been thinking about this all afternoon."

"Actually," I said, pleased that I was able to answer this one truthfully. "I really haven't. Now get off me."

But Paul just went on kissing me—not on the mouth, because I had fully turned my head away, but on my neck and, at one point, part of one of my ears.

"Is this about the student government thing?" he asked between kisses. "Because I could care less about being vice president of your stupid class. If you're mad about it, just say the word, and I'll drop out of the race."

"No, this has nothing to do with the student government thing," I said, still trying to wrench my wrist from his fingers and also to keep my neck away from his mouth. His lips seemed to have a curious effect on the skin of my throat. They made it feel like it was on fire.

"Oh, God. It's not Jesse, is it?" I could feel Paul's groan reverberate through his entire body. "Give it up, Suze. The guy's *dead*."

"I didn't say it had anything to do with Jesse." I sounded defensive, but I didn't care. "Did you hear me say it had anything to do with Jesse?"

"You didn't have to," Paul said. "It's written all over your face. Suze, think about it. Where's it going to go with the guy, anyway? I mean, you're going to get older, and he's going to stay exactly the age he was when he croaked. And what, he's going to take you to the prom? How about movies? You guys go to the movies together? Who drives? Who *pays*?"

Now I was really mad at him. More, of course, because he was right than anything else. Also because he was assuming that Jesse even returned my feelings, which sadly, I knew was not true. Why else would he have stayed away from me so assiduously these past few weeks?

Then Paul plunged the knife deeper.

"Besides, if the two of you were really right for each other, would you even be here? And would you have been kissing me like you were a minute ago?"

That did it. Now I was furious. Because he was right. That was the thing. He was right.

And it was breaking my heart. Worse than Jesse already had.

"If you don't get off me," I said, through gritted teeth, "I will jab my thumb into your eye socket."

Paul chuckled. Although I noticed he stopped chuckling when my thumb did actually meet with the corner of his eye.

"Ow!" he yelled, rolling off me fast. "What the—"

I was up and off that bed faster than you could say paranormal activity. I grabbed my shoes, my bag, and what was left of my dignity, and got the heck out of there.

"Suze!" Paul yelled from his bedroom. "Get back here! Suze!"

I didn't pay any attention. I just kept on running. I tore past Grandpa Slater's room—he was still watching an old rerun of *Family Feud*—then started down the twisting staircase to the front door.

I would have made it, too, if a three-hundred-pound Hell's Angel hadn't suddenly materialized between me and the door.

That's right. One minute my way was clear, and the next it was blocked by Biker Bob. Or should I say, the ghost of Biker Bob.

"Whoa," I said, as I nearly barreled into him.

The guy had a handlebar mustache and heavily tattooed arms, which he had crossed in front of him. He was also, I shouldn't need to point out, quite, quite dead. "Where'd *you* come from?"

"Never you mind that, little lady," he said. "I think Mr. Slater'd still like a word with you."

I heard footsteps at the top of the stairs and looked up. Paul was there, one hand still over his eye.

"Suze," he said. "Don't go."

"*Minions*?" I called up to him incredulously. "You have ghostly *minions* to do your bidding? What *are* you?"

"I told you," Paul said. "I'm a shifter. So are you. And you are way overreacting about this whole thing. Can't we just talk, Suze? I swear I'll keep my hands to myself."

"Where have I heard that before?" I asked.

Then, as Biker Bob took a threatening step toward me, I did the only thing that, under the circumstances, I felt that I could. I lifted up one of my Jimmy Choos and smacked him in the head with it.

This is not, I am sure, the purpose for which Mr. Choo designed that particular mule. It did, however, work quite handily. With a very surprised Biker Bob incapacitated, it was only a matter of shoving him out of the way, throwing open the door, and making a run for it. Which I did, with alacrity.

I was tearing down the long cement steps from Paul's front door to his driveway when I heard him calling after me, "Suze! Suze, come on. I'm sorry for what I said about Jesse. I didn't mean it."

I turned in the driveway to face him. I am sorry to say that I responded to his statement by making a rude, single-fingered gesture.

"Suze." Paul had taken his hand down from his face, so that I could see that his eye was not, as I had hoped, dangling out of its socket. It just looked red. "At least let me drive you home."

"No, thank you," I called to him, pausing to slip on my Jimmy Choos. "I prefer to walk."

"Suze," Paul said. "It's like five miles from here to your house."

"Never speak to me again, please," I said, and started walking, hoping he wouldn't try to follow me. Because of course if he did, and attempted to kiss me again, there was a very good chance I would kiss him back. I knew that now. Knew it only too well.

He didn't follow me. I made it down his driveway and out onto the oceanfront road—imaginatively named Scenic Drive—with what was left of my self-esteem still more or less intact. It wasn't until I was out of sight of Paul's house that I yanked off my shoes and said what I'd wanted to say the whole time I'd been striding, with as much hauteur as I could, away from him. Which was, "Ouch, ouch, ouch!"

Stupid shoes. My toes were in shreds. No way could I walk in the torturous mules. I thought about flinging them into the ocean, which would have been easy considering it was below me.

On the other hand, the shoes were six hundred bucks, retail. Granted I had gotten them for a fraction of that, but still. The shopaholic in me would not allow so rash a move.

So, holding my shoes in my hand, I began to mince my way down the road barefoot, keeping a sharp eye out for bits of glass and any poison oak that might be growing alongside the street.

Paul had been right about one thing: it was a five-mile walk from his house to mine. Worse, it was about a mile walk from his house to the first commercial structure at which I might reason-ably expect to find a pay phone where I could start calling around to see if I could get someone to pick me up. I could, I supposed, have gone up to one of the huge houses belonging to Paul's neighbors, rung the bell, and asked if I could use their phone. But how embarrassing would that be? No, a pay phone. That was all I needed. And I'd find one, soon enough.

There was only one real flaw in my plan, and that was the weather. Oh, don't get me wrong. It was a beautiful September day. There wasn't a cloud in the sky.

That was the problem. The sun was beating down mercilessly upon Scenic Drive. It had to have been ninety degrees at least—even though the cool breeze from the sea didn't make it seem uncomfortable. But the pavement beneath my bare feet wasn't affected by the breeze. The road, which had seemed comfortably warm beneath the soles of my feet when I'd first come barreling out of Paul's cold, cold house, was actually extremely hot. Burning hot. Like fry-an-egg-on-it hot.

There wasn't anything I could do about it, of course. I couldn't put my shoes back on. My blisters hurt more than the soles of my feet. Maybe if a car had gone by, I'd have tried to flag it down— but probably not. I was too embarrassed by my predicament, really, to have to explain it to a total stranger. Besides, given my luck, I'd probably manage to flag down a serial killer and find myself out of the frying pan—literally—and smack in the middle of the fire.

No. I kept walking, cursing myself and my stupidity. How could I have been so dumb as to have agreed to go to Paul Slater's house? True, the stuff he'd showed me about the shifters had been interesting. And that thing about soul transference . . . if there really was such a thing. I didn't even want to let myself think about what *that* might mean. To put a soul in someone else's body.

Shifting, I said to myself. Concentrate on the whole shifting thing. Better that, of course, than on the soul transference thing . . . or worse, the even more unpleasant topic of how I could be so carried away by the kisses of someone other than the guy I happened to be in love with.

Or was it just that, after Jesse's seeming rejection, I was simply relieved to find that I was attractive to somebody . . . even somebody whom I did not particularly like? Because I did not like Paul Slater. I did not. I think the fact that I had been having bad dreams about him for the past few weeks was proof enough of that . . . no matter how fast my traitorous heart might beat when his lips were pressed against mine.

It felt good, as I walked, to concentrate on this instead of my extremely sore feet. It was slow going, walking down Scenic Drive without any protection from the shards of gravel and, of course, the hot pavement beneath my soles. Of course, in a way I felt that the pain was punishment for my very bad behavior. True, Paul had lured me to his house with promises that he would reveal some information I had very badly wanted. But I ought to have resisted just the same, knowing that someone like Paul would have to have a hidden agenda.

And that that agenda would most likely involve my mouth.

What galled me was that for a minute or so back there, I hadn't cared. Really. I'd *liked* it, even. Bad Suze. *Very* bad Suze.

Oh, God. I was in trouble.

Then, finally, after about half an hour of painful mincing, I saw the most beautiful sight in the world: a seaside café. I hurried toward it—well, as fast as I could on feet that felt as if they had been hacked off at the ankle—mentally ticking off who I could safely call when I got there. My mom? Never. She'd ask too many questions and probably kill me besides for agreeing to go to the house of a boy she'd never met. Jake? No. Again, he'd ask too many questions. Brad? No, he would just as soon leave me stranded, as he happened to hate my guts. Adam?

It was going to have to be Adam. He was the only person I knew who would not only happily drive out to get me but who would relish his role as rescuer . . . not to mention also greatly enjoy hearing about how Paul had sexually harassed me without afterward desiring to beat Paul into a bloody pulp. Adam would have the sense to know that Paul Slater could kick his ass any day of the week. I would not mention to Adam, of course, the part where I'd sexually harassed Paul right back.

The Sea Mist Café—that was the restaurant I was limping toward—was an upscale restaurant with outdoor seating and valet parking. It was too late for lunch and too early for it to be serving dinner, so there were no diners there, just the wait staff, setting up for the supper rush. As I came hobbling up, a waiter was just writing the specials on the chalkboard by the door.

"Hey," I said to him in my brightest, least look-at-me-I-am-a-victim voice.

The waiter glanced at me. If he noticed my disheveled, shoeless appearance, he did not comment upon it. He turned back to his chalkboard.

"We don't start seating for dinner until six," he said.

"Um." This was, I saw, going to be more difficult than I'd thought. "That's fine. I just want to use your pay phone, if you have one."

"Inside," the waiter said with a sigh. Then, his gaze flicking over me scathingly, he added, "No shoes, no service."

"I've got shoes," I said, holding up my Jimmy Choos. "See?"

He rolled his eyes and turned back to his chalk-board.

I don't know why the world has to be populated by so many unpleasant people. I really don't. It really takes an effort to be rude, too. The amount of energy people expend on being a jerk astounds me sometimes.

Inside the Sea Mist, it was cool and shady. I limped past the bar toward the little sign I'd seen, as soon as my eyes adjusted to the dim light— compared to the blazing sun outside—that said PHONE/RESTROOMS. It was sort of a long walk to the Phone/Restrooms for a girl with what I was pretty sure were massive third-degree burns on the soles of her feet. I had gotten halfway there when I heard a guy's voice say my name.

I was sure it was Paul. I mean, who else could it have been? Paul had followed me from his house and wanted to apologize.

And probably make out some more.

Well, if he thought I was going to forgive him—
let alone kiss him again—he had another think
coming, let me tell you. Well, actually, maybe the
kissing part—

No. *No.*

I turned around slowly.

"I told you," I said, keeping my voice even
with an effort. "I don't ever want to speak to you
again. . . ."

My voice trailed off. It wasn't Paul Slater standing behind me. It was Jake's friend from college,
Neil Jankow. Neil Jankow, Craig's brother, standing
there by the bar with a clipboard, looking thinner
than ever . . . and now that I knew what he'd been
through, sadder than ever, too.

"Susan?" he said, hesitantly. "Oh, it is you. I
wasn't sure."

I blinked at him. And his clipboard. And the
bartender who was standing near him, holding a
similar clipboard. Then I remembered what Neil
had said, about his dad owning a lot of restaurants in Carmel. Craig and Neil Jankow's father, I
realized, must own the Sea Mist Café.

"Neil," I said. "Hi. Yeah, it's me, Suze. How . . .
um, how are you doing?"

"I'm fine," Neil said, his gaze going to my
extremely dirty feet. "Are you . . . are you all right?"

The concern in his voice was, I knew immediately, actually heartfelt. Neil Jankow was worried about me. Me, a girl whom he'd met only the night before. Whose name he hadn't even gotten right. The fact that he could be so concerned about me while other people—namely Paul Slater, and yes, I was willing to admit it now, Jesse—could be so very, very mean, brought tears to my eyes.

"I'm okay," I said.

And then, before I could stop it, the whole story came pouring out. Nothing about the ghosts and the whole mediator thing, of course. But the rest of it, anyway. I don't know what came over me. I was just standing there in the middle of Neil's dad's café, going, "And then he made a move on me, and I told him to get off and he wouldn't so I had to jab my thumb in his eye, and then I ran away but my shoes really hurt and so I had to take them off and I don't have a cell phone so I couldn't call anyone and this is the first place with a pay phone that I could find—"

Before I'd finished, Neil was at my side, steering me toward the closest bar stool and making me sit on it. He said, "Hey. Hey, it's all right now," all nervously. It was clear he didn't have a whole lot of experience dealing with hysterical girls. He kept patting my shoulder and offering me things, like free lemonade and tiramisu.

"I'll . . . I'll take some lemonade," I said, finally, worn down from my recital of woes.

"Sure," Neil said. "Sure thing. Jorge, get her some lemonade, will you?"

The bartender hurried to pour me some lemonade from a pitcher he kept in a little fridge behind the bar. He put it in front of me, eyeing me warily, like I was some lunatic who might start spouting off New Age poetry at any minute. It was heartening to know this was the first impression I was giving people. Not.

I drank some of the lemonade. It was cool and tart. I put the glass down after a few gulps and said to Neil, who was looking at me with concern, "Thanks. I feel better. You're nice."

Neil looked embarrassed. "Um. Thanks. Look, I have a cell phone. Do you want to borrow it? You can call someone. Maybe you could call, you know, Jake."

Jake? Oh, God no. My eyes wide, I shook my head. "No," I said. "Not Jake. He . . . he wouldn't understand."

Neil was beginning to look panicky. You could tell all he wanted was to get rid of me. And who could blame him, really? "Oh, okay. Your mom, then? How about your mom?"

I shook my head some more. "No, no. I don't . . . I mean, I don't want them to know how stupid I was."

Jorge, the bartender, went, "You know, we're pretty much done here, Neil. You can go, if you want. . . . "

And take her with you. He didn't say the words, but his tone implied them. It was clear that Jorge wanted the crazy girl with the sore feet out of his bar, and pronto . . . like before the first customers of the evening started to trickle in.

Neil looked pained. It was very gratifying to know that my appearance was so heinous at that moment, that college boys hesitated to allow me into their vehicles. Really. I can't tell you how much I appreciated that fact. Bad enough I was jailbait, but I also appeared to be jailbait with bloody feet and a wicked case of the frizzies, thanks to the salt air.

Neil, who'd had his cell phone out, closed it and stuck it back in the pocket of his Dockers.

"Um," he said. "I guess, you know. I could drive you home myself. If you want."

The delivery left a little to be desired, but I

don't think I could have been more grateful, even if he'd said he knew a place that sold Prada wholesale.

"That would be so, so great," I gushed.

I guess my gushing was a little too effusive, since Neil's face turned as pink as my blisters, and he hurried away. Mumbling about how he just had to finish up a few things. I didn't care. Home! I was getting a ride home! No embarrassing phone calls, no more walking . . . Oh, thank God, no more walking. I don't think I could have stood on my feet for another minute. Just looking down at them made me feel a little light-headed. They were almost black with dirt, and let's just say the Band-Aids had taken a licking, and sure weren't doing much sticking. Lovely oozing sores gleamed redly at me. I didn't even want to look at what was going on with the soles of my feet. All I knew was that I couldn't feel them anymore. They were completely numb.

"That," observed a voice at my elbow, "is one wicked pedicure. You should ask for your money back."

chapter *ten*

I didn't even have to turn my head to see who it was.

"Hi, Craig," I said out of the corner of my mouth. Neil and Jorge were too deeply absorbed in the beverage order they were just finishing up discussing to pay attention to me, anyway.

"So." Craig settled onto the bar stool next to mine. "This is how you mediators work? Get your feet all wrecked, then mooch rides off the siblings of the deceased?"

"Not usually," I murmured discreetly.

"Oh." Craig fiddled with a book of matches from the bar. "Because I was going to say. You know. Great technique. Really making some stellar progress on my case there, aren't you?"

I sighed. Really, after everything I'd been through, I did not need some dead guy making wisecracks.

But I guess I deserved them.

"How are you doing?" I asked, trying to keep my tone light. "You know, with the whole being dead thing?"

"Oh, jim-dandy," Craig said. "Loving every minute of it."

"You'll get used to it," I said, thinking of Jesse.

"Oh, I'm sure I will," Craig said. He was looking at Neil.

I should, of course, have gotten a clue then. But I didn't. I was too caught up in my own problems . . . not to mention my feet.

Then Neil handed his clipboard to Jorge, shook his hand, and turned to me.

"Are you ready, Susan?" he asked.

I didn't bother to correct him about my name. I just nodded and slid down from the bar stool. I had to look to make sure my feet had hit the floor, because I couldn't feel it. The floor, I mean. The skin on the bottoms of my feet had gone completely numb.

"You really did a number on yourself," was Craig's comment.

But he, unlike his brother, very helpfully slipped an arm around my waist and guided me toward the door, where Neil was waiting, his car keys in his hand.

I must have looked particularly peculiar as I approached—I was definitely leaning some of my weight into Craig, which must have given me an odd appearance, since of course Neil couldn't see Craig—because Neil said, "Um, Susan, are you sure you want to go straight home? I think maybe you might want to pay a little visit to the emergency room. . . ."

"No, no," I said lightly. "I'm fine."

"Right," Craig snickered in my ear.

Still, with his help, I made it out to Neil's car all right. Like Paul, Neil had a convertible BMW. Unlike Paul's, Neil's appeared to be secondhand.

"Hey!" Craig cried, when he saw the vehicle. "That's *my* car!"

This was, I felt, the natural reaction of a guy who'd found his car in the possession of another. Jake would undoubtedly have said the same thing. Over and over again.

Craig got over his indignation long enough to steer me into the front seat. I was about to give him a grateful smile when he then hopped into the backseat. Even then, of course, I didn't figure it out. I just assumed Craig wanted to come along for the ride. Why not? It wasn't like he had anything better to do, so far as I knew.

Neil started the engine, and Kylie Minogue began to wail from his CD player.

"I can't believe he's listening to this garbage," Craig said disgustedly from the backseat, "in *my* car."

"I like her," I said, a little defensively.

Neil looked at me. "You say something?"

Realizing what I'd done, I said no quickly.

"Oh."

Without another word—he wasn't apparently much of a conversationalist—Neil pulled his car out from the Sea Mist Café parking lot and headed down Scenic Drive for downtown Carmel, which we'd have to cut through to make it back to my house. Cutting through downtown Carmel was never a picnic, because it was usually crammed with tourists and the tourists never knew where they were going, because none of the streets had names . . . or stoplights.

But it can be especially dangerous navigating downtown Carmel-by-the-Sea when there happens to be a homicidal ghost in your backseat.

I didn't realize this right away, of course. I was attempting to do some, you know, mediation. I figured, as long as I had the two brothers together, I might as well try to patch things up between them. I had no idea at the time just how badly their relationship had disintegrated, of course.

"So, Neil," I said conversationally, as we went down Scenic Drive at a pretty good clip. The ocean breeze tugged at my hair and felt deliciously cool after the way the sun had beat down on me earlier. "I heard about your brother. I'm really sorry."

Neil didn't take his gaze off the road. But I saw his fingers tighten on the steering wheel.

"Thanks," was all he said in a quiet voice.

It is generally considered rude to pry into the personal tragedies of others—particularly when the victims of said tragedy were not the ones who introduced the subject—but for a mediator, being rude is all part of the job. I said, "It must have been really awful, out there on that boat."

"Catamaran," both Craig and Neil corrected me at the same time—Craig derisively, Neil gently.

"I mean catamaran," I said. "How long did you hang on for, anyway? Like eight hours or something?"

"Seven," Neil said softly.

"Seven hours," I said. "That's a long time. The water must have been really cold."

"It was," Neil said. He was clearly a man of few words. I did not allow that to dissuade me from my mission, however.

"And I understand," I said, "that your brother was what, a champion swimmer or something?"

"Damned straight," Craig said from the backseat. "Made all-state—"

I held up a hand to silence him. It was not Craig I wanted to hear from just then.

"Champion swimmer," Neil said, his voice not much louder than the purr of the BMW's engine. "Champion sailor. You name it, Craig was better at it than anybody."

"See?" Craig leaned forward. "See? *He's* the one that should be dead. Not me. He even admits it!"

"Shhh," I said to Craig. To Neil I said, "That must have really surprised people, then. I mean, when you survived the accident, and Craig didn't."

"Disappointed them, is more like it," Neil muttered. Still, I heard him.

So did Craig.

He settled back against the seat, looking triumphant. "I told you so."

"I'm sure your parents are sad about losing Craig," I said, ignoring the ghost in the backseat. "And you're going to have to give them some time. But they're happy not to have lost you, Neil. You know they are."

"They aren't," Neil said as matter-of-factly as if he'd been saying the sky is blue. "They liked Craig better. Everybody did. I know what they're thinking. What everybody is thinking. That it should have been me. I should have been the one to die. Not Craig."

Craig leaned forward again. "See?" he said. "Even Neil admits it. He should be the one back here, not me."

But I was now more concerned for the living brother than I was for the dead one. "Neil, you can't mean that."

"Why not?" Neil shrugged. "It's the truth."

"It's not true," I said. "There's a reason you lived and Craig didn't."

"Yeah," Craig said sarcastically. "Somebody messed up. Big time."

"No," I said, shaking my head. "That's not it. Craig hit his head. Plain and simple. It was an accident, Neil. An accident that wasn't your fault."

Neil looked, for a moment, like someone upon whom the sun had begun to shine after months of rain . . . like he hardly dared believe it.

"Do you really think so?" he asked eagerly.

"Absolutely," I said. "That's all there is to it."

But while this news appeared to have made Neil's day—possibly his week—it caused Craig to scowl.

"What is this?" he wanted to know. "He should have died! Not me!"

"Apparently not," I said quietly enough so that only Craig could hear me.

This, however, did not prove to be the right answer. Not because it wasn't true—because it was—but because Craig did not like it. Craig did not like it one little bit.

"If I have to be dead," Craig declared, "then so should *he*."

And with that, he lunged forward and seized the steering wheel.

Neil was driving down a particularly quaint street, shady with trees and crowded with tourists. Art galleries and quilt shops—the kind my mother squealed over delightedly, and that I avoided like the plague—lined it. We were crawling along at a snail's pace because there was an RV in front of us and a tourist bus in front of that.

But when Craig grabbed the wheel, the back of the RV suddenly loomed large in our field of vision. That's because Craig also managed to bring a leg over the backseat, and rammed his foot over Neil's on the accelerator, something Neil couldn't feel. All he knew was *he* hadn't pressed the gas pedal. If Neil hadn't reacted by slamming on the brake with his other foot—and I hadn't dived into the fray, yanking the wheel hard back the other way—we would have zoomed into the rear of that RV—or worse, into a thick knot of tourists on the sidewalk—killing ourselves, not to mention taking a few innocent bystanders out with us.

"What is *wrong* with you?" I shrieked at Craig.

But it was Neil who responded shakily, "It wasn't me, I swear. The wheel just seemed to turn without my doing anything. . . ."

But I wasn't listening. I was screaming at Craig, who seemed as stunned as Neil was by what had transpired. He kept looking down at his hands, like they had acted of their own volition or something.

"Don't you ever," I yelled at him, "do that again. Not ever! Do you understand?"

"I'm sorry," Neil cried. "But it wasn't my fault, I swear it!"

Craig, with a pitiful little moan, suddenly gave a shimmer and disappeared. Just like that. He dematerialized, leaving Neil and me to deal with his mess.

Which fortunately wasn't that bad. I mean, a lot of people were looking at us, because we had stopped in the middle of the street and done a lot of screaming and yelling. But neither of us was hurt—nor, mercifully, was anyone else. We hadn't so much as tapped the back of the RV. A second later, it started rolling forward, and we followed it, our hearts in our throats.

"I better take this car in for an overhaul," Neil said, clutching the steering wheel with white-knuckled fingers. "Maybe the oil needs to be changed or something."

"Or something," I said. My heart was drumming in my ears. "That'd be a good idea. Maybe you should start taking the bus for a little while." Or until I figure out what to do about your brother, I added mentally.

"Yeah," Neil said faintly. "The bus might not be so bad."

I don't know about Neil, but I was still somewhat shaken by the time he pulled up in front of my house. I had had quite a day. It wasn't often I got French-kissed and nearly murdered in the course of only a few hours.

Still, in spite of my own unease, I wanted to say something to Neil, something that would encourage him not to be so depressed over his being the sibling who'd lived . . . and also set him on his guard against his brother, who had seemed angrier than ever when he'd disappeared minutes earlier.

But all I could come up with, when it came down to it, was a very lame, "Well. Thanks for the ride."

Really. That was it. *Thanks for the ride*. No wonder I was winning all those mediation awards. Not.

Neil didn't look as if he was paying much attention anyway. He seemed to just want to get rid of me. And why not? I mean, what college boy wants to be saddled with a crazy-looking high school girl with giant blisters on her feet? None that I know of.

The minute I'd stepped from the car, he tore down our deeply shaded, pine-tree-lined driveway, apparently unconcerned about the accident he'd nearly suffered just moments before.

Or maybe he was so glad to be rid of me, he didn't care what happened to him or his car.

All I know is, he was gone, leaving me with the long, long walk up to my front door.

I don't know how I made it. I really don't. But going slowly—as slowly as a very, very old woman—I made it up the stairs to the porch, then through the front door.

"I'm home," I yelled, in case there was anybody around who'd care. Only Max came running to greet me, sniffing me all over in hopes I had food hidden in my pockets. Since I didn't, he soon went away, leaving me to make my way up the stairs to my room.

I did it, step by agonizing step. It took me, I don't know, like ten minutes or something. Normally I bound up and down two steps at a time. Not today.

I was, I knew, going to have a lot of explaining to do when I finally ran into someone besides Max. But the person I least wanted to have to face was going to be, I felt certain, the first person I'd see: Jesse. Jesse would be, more likely than not, in my room when I hobbled through the door. Jesse, who was not going to understand what I was doing at Paul Slater's house in the first place. Jesse, from whom I thought it was going to be difficult to hide the fact that I had just been playing tonsil hockey with another guy.

And that I'd sort of liked it.

It was, I told myself as I stood with my hand on the doorknob, Jesse's fault. That I'd gone off and made out with another guy. Because if Jesse had shown me the slightest shred of affection these past few weeks, I would never even have considered kissing Paul Slater back. Not in a million years.

Yeah, that was it. It was all *Jesse's* fault.

Not that I was ever going to tell *him* that, of course. In fact, if I could possibly avoid it, I was going to keep from bringing up Paul's name altogether. I needed to think up some story—any story, other than the truth—to explain my poor, abused feet . . .

. . . not to mention my bruised lips.

But to my relief, when I threw open the door to my room, Jesse wasn't there. Spike was, sitting on the windowsill, washing himself. But not his master. Not this time.

Alleluia.

I threw down my book bag and shoes and headed to my bathroom. I had one thing, and one thing only on my mind, and that was to wash my feet. Maybe all they needed was a thorough cleaning. Maybe, if I soaked them long enough in warm, soapy water, some of the feeling in them would come back. . . .

I opened the taps full blast, put the stopper in place, and sitting on the edge of the tub, swung my legs painfully over it and into the water.

It was all right for a second or two. In fact, it was a soothing relief.

Then the water hit my blisters, and I nearly keeled over with the pain. *Never again*, I vowed, clutching the side of the tub in an effort not to pass out. No more designer shoes. From now on, it was strictly Aerosoles for me. I don't care how ugly they might look. Not even looking good was worth this.

The pain ebbed enough for me to make a tentative foray with a bar of Cetaphil and a sponge. It wasn't until I had gently scrubbed for nearly five minutes before I got through the final layer of dirt and saw why the bottoms of my feet were so desensitized. Because they were covered— literally covered—with giant red burn blisters, some of them blood filled and all of them getting bigger by the minute. I realized, with horror, that it was going to be days—maybe even a week— before the swelling was going to go down enough for me to walk normally again, let alone put on shoes.

I was sitting there cursing Paul Slater—not to mention Jimmy Choo—for all I was worth when I heard Jesse utter a curse that, even though it was in Spanish, burned my ears.

chapter *eleven*

"*Querida*, what have you done to yourself?"

Jesse stood at the side of the tub looking down at my feet. I had drained out all the dirty water and had run a new tubful to soak them in, so it was pretty easy to see through the clear water to the angry red blisters below it.

"New shoes," I said. It was all the explanation I was capable of thinking up at the moment. The fact that I had had to flee in my bare feet from a sexual predator did not seem like the kind of thing that would sit too well with Jesse. I mean, I didn't exactly want to be the cause of any duels or anything.

Yeah, yeah, I know: I wish.

Still, he'd called me *querida* again. That had to mean something, right?

Except that Jesse had probably called his sisters *querida*. Possibly even his mom.

"You did that to yourself on *purpose*?" Jesse was staring down at my feet in utter disbelief.

"Well," I said. "Not exactly." Only instead of telling him about Paul, and our clandestine kisses on his dark-gray bedspread, I said, talking about a hundred miles a minute, "It's just that they were new shoes, and they gave me blisters and then . . . and then I missed my ride home, and I had to walk, and my shoes hurt so much I took them off, and I guess the pavement was hot from the sun, since I burned the bottoms of my feet—"

Jesse looked grim. He sat on the edge of the tub beside me and said, "Let me see."

I didn't want to show the guy with whom I have been madly in love since the very first day I met him my hideously disfigured feet. I especially didn't want him to see them considering that he didn't know that I had burned them in an effort to get away from a guy I shouldn't have been with in the first place.

On the other hand, you should be able to go over to boys' houses without them jumping on you and kissing you and making you want to kiss them back. It was all sort of complicated, even to me, and I am a modern young woman with twenty-first-century sensibilities. God only knew what a rancher from the 1850s would make of it all.

But I could see by Jesse's expression that he was not going to leave me alone until I showed him my stupid feet. So I said, rolling my eyes, "You want to see them? Fine. Knock yourself out."

And I pulled my right foot from the water and showed him.

I expected, at the very least, some revulsion. Chastisement for my stupidity, I felt quite sure, would soon follow—as if I didn't feel stupid enough.

But to my surprise, Jesse neither chastised me nor looked revolted. He merely examined my foot with what I would have to describe as almost clinical detachment. When he was through looking at my right foot, he said, "Let me see the other one."

So I put the right one back in the water and pulled out the left one.

Again, no revulsion and no cries of "Suze, how could you be so stupid?" Which wasn't actually that surprising, since Jesse never calls me Suze. Instead, he examined my left foot as carefully as he had the other one. When he was through, he leaned back and said, "Well, I have seen worse . . . but barely."

I was shocked by this.

"You've seen feet that looked worse than *this*?" I cried. *"Where?"*

"I had sisters, remember?" he said, his dark eyes alight with something—I wouldn't have called it amusement, because of course my feet weren't a laughing matter. Jesse wouldn't dare laugh at them . . . would he? "Occasionally they got new shoes, with similar results."

"I'll never walk again, will I?" I asked, looking woefully down at my ravaged feet.

"You will," Jesse said. "Just not for a day or two. Those burns look very painful. They'll need butter."

"Butter?" I wrinkled my nose.

"The best treatment for burns like those is butter," Jesse said.

"Uh," I said. "Maybe back in 1850. Now we tend to rely on the healing power of Neosporin. There's a tube of it in my medicine cabinet behind you."

So Jesse applied Neosporin to my wounds.

I was deeply absorbed in my essay on the Civil War—or at least, that's what I was pretending to be doing. What I was really doing, of course, was trying not to think about Jesse, who was over on the window seat reading. I was wondering what it would be like if he laid a couple of kisses like Paul's on me. I mean, if you thought about it, he had me in a really interesting position, considering that I couldn't walk. How many guys would have loved to have a girl basically trapped in her bedroom? A lot of them. Except, of course, for Jesse. Finally Andy called me down to dinner.

I wasn't going anywhere, however. Not because I wanted to stick around and watch Jesse read some more, but because I really couldn't stand. Finally David came upstairs to see what was taking me so long. As soon as he saw the Band-Aids, he went running back downstairs for my mom.

May I just say that my mother was a good deal less sympathetic than Jesse? She said I deserved every blister for being so asinine as to wear new shoes to school without breaking them in first. Then she fussed around my room, straightening it up (although since acquiring a roommate of the hot Latino male persuasion, I have become quite conscientious about keeping my room in a fairly neat condition. I mean, I don't exactly want

Jesse seeing any of my stray bras lying around. And really, if anything, he was the one who was always messing things up, leaving these enormous piles of books and open CD cases everywhere. And then of course there was Spike).

"Honestly, Susie," my mom said, wrinkling her nose at the sight of the big orange tabby sprawled out on my window seat. "That cat . . ."

Jesse, who had politely dematerialized when my mom showed up, in order to afford me some modicum of privacy, would have been greatly disturbed to hear his pet disparaged so.

"How's the patient?" Andy wanted to know, appearing in my doorway with a dinner tray containing grilled salmon with dill and crème fraîche, cold cucumber soup, and a freshly baked sourdough dinner roll. You know, unhappy as I'd been at the prospect of my mom remarrying and forcing me to move all the way across the country and acquire three stepbrothers, I had to admit, the food made it all worth it.

Well, the food and Jesse. At least up until recently.

"She's definitely not going to be able to go to school tomorrow," my mom said, shaking her head despairingly at the sight of my feet. "I mean, look at them, Andy. Do you think we need to take her to . . . I don't know . . . PromptCare, or something?"

Andy bent down and looked at my feet. "I don't know that they could do anything more," he said, admiring Jesse's excellent bandaging job. "Looks like she's taken pretty good care of it herself."

"You know what I probably do need," I said. "Some magazines and a six-pack of Diet Coke and one of those really big Crunch bars."

"Don't push it, young lady," my mom said severely. "You are not going to loll around in bed all day tomorrow like some kind of injured ballerina. I am going to call Mr. Walden tonight and make sure he gets you all of your homework. And I have to say, Susie, I am very disappointed in you. You are too old for this kind of nonsense. You could have called me at the station, you know. I would have come out to get you."

Uh, yeah. And then she would have found out that I was walking home not from school, like I'd told everyone, but from the home of a guy who had a dead Hell's Angel working for him and who had, oh yeah, tried to put the moves on me with his drooling grandpa right in the next room. Moves I had, at least up to a point, reciprocated.

No, thanks.

I overheard Andy, as the two of them left my

room, say softly to my mom, "Don't you think you were a little hard on her? I think she learned her lesson."

My mom, however, didn't answer Andy back softly at all. No, she wanted me to hear her reply: "No, I do not think I was too hard on her. She'll be leaving for college in two years, Andy, and living on her own. If this is an example of the kinds of decisions she'll be making then, I shudder to think what lies ahead. In fact, I'm thinking we should cancel our plans to go away Friday night."

"Not on your life," I heard Andy say very emphatically from the bottom of the stairs.

"But—"

"No buts," Andy said. "We're going."

And then I couldn't hear them anymore.

Jesse, who rematerialized at the end of all of this, had a little smile on his face, having clearly overheard.

"It isn't funny," I said to him sourly.

"It's a little funny," he said.

"No," I said, "it isn't."

"I think," Jesse said, cracking open the book Father Dom had loaned him, "it's time for a little reading out loud."

"No," I groaned. "Not *Critical Theory Since*

Plato. Please, I am begging you. It's not fair, I can't even run away."

"I know," Jesse said with a gleam in his eyes. "At last I have you where I want you. . . ."

I have to admit, my breath kind of caught in my throat when he said that.

But of course he didn't mean what I *wanted* him to mean. He just meant that now he could read his stupid book out loud, and I couldn't escape.

"Ha-ha," I said wittily, to cover the fact that I thought he had meant something else.

Then Jesse held up a copy of *Cosmo* he'd hidden between the pages of *Critical Theory Since Plato*. While I stared at him in astonishment, he said, "I borrowed it from your mother's room. She won't miss it for a while."

Then he tossed the magazine onto my bed.

I nearly choked. I mean, it was the nicest—the *nicest*—thing anyone had done for me in ages. And the fact that Jesse—Jesse, whom I'd become convinced lately hated me—had done it, positively floored me. Was it possible that he didn't hate me? Was it possible that, in fact, he *liked* me a little? I mean, I know Jesse *likes* me. Why else would he always be saving my life and all? But was it possible he liked me in that *special* way? Or was he only being nice to me on account of the fact that I was injured?

It didn't matter. Not just then, anyway. The fact that Jesse wasn't ignoring me for a change—whatever his motive—was all that mattered.

Happily, I began to read an article about seven ways to please a man, and didn't even mind so much that I didn't have one—a man, I mean, of my very own. Because at last it seemed that whatever weirdness had existed between Jesse and me since the day of that kiss—that all too brief, sense-shattering kiss—was going away. Maybe now things would get back to normal. Maybe now he'd start to realize how stupid he'd been. Maybe now he'd finally get it through his head that he needed me. More than needed me. Wanted me.

As much, I now knew in no uncertain terms, as Paul Slater did.

Hey, a girl can dream, right?

And that was exactly what I did. For eighteen blissful hours, I dreamed of a life where the guy I liked actually liked me back. I put all thoughts of mediation—shifting and soul transference, Paul Slater and Father Dominic, Craig and Neil Jankow—from my mind. The last part was easy— I asked Jesse to keep an eye on Craig for me, and he happily agreed to do so.

And I won't lie to you: It was great. No nightmares about being chased down long, fog-enshrouded hallways toward a bottomless drop-off. Yeah, it wasn't quite like the old, prekiss days, but it came close. Sort of. Until the next day when the phone rang.

I picked it up, and CeeCee's voice shrieked at me, loudly enough that I had to hold the receiver away from my head.

"I cannot believe you decided to take a sick day," CeeCee ranted. "Today, of all days! How could you, Suze? We have so much campaigning to do!"

It took me a few seconds before I realized what she was talking about. Then I went, "Oh, you mean the election? CeeCee, look, I—"

"I mean, you should see what Kelly's doing. She's handing out candy bars—candy bars—that say *Vote Prescott/Slater* on the wrappers! Okay? And what are you doing? Oh, lolling around in bed because your feet hurt, if what your brother says is true."

"Stepbrother," I corrected her.

"Whatever. Suze, you can't do this to me. I don't care what you do—put on some fuzzy bunny slippers if you have to—just get here and be your usual charming self."

"CeeCee," I said. It was kind of hard to concentrate because Jesse was nearby. Not just nearby, but touching me. And okay, only putting more Band-Aids on my feet, but it was still way distracting. "Look. I'm pretty sure I don't want to be vice president—"

But CeeCee didn't want to hear it.

"Suze," she yelled into Adam's cell phone. I knew she was using Adam's cell phone and that she was on her lunch break, because I could hear the sound of gulls screaming—gulls flock to the school assembly yard during lunch, hoping to score a dropped French fry or two—and I could also hear Adam in the background cheering her on. "It is bad enough that Kelly Mousse-for-Brains Prescott gets elected president of our class every year. But at least when you got elected vice president last year, some semblance of dignity was accorded to the office. But if that blue-eyed rich boy gets elected—I mean, he is just Kelly's pawn. He doesn't care. He'll do whatever Kelly says."

CeeCee had one thing right: Paul didn't care. Not about the junior class at the Junipero Serra Mission Academy, anyway. I wasn't sure just what, exactly, Paul did care about, since it certainly wasn't his family or mediating. But one thing he definitely was not going to do was take his position as vice president very seriously.

"Listen, CeeCee," I said. "I'm really sorry. But I truly did screw up my feet, and I really can't walk. Maybe tomorrow."

"Tomorrow?" CeeCee squawked. "The election's Friday! That gives us only one full day to campaign!"

"Well," I said, "maybe you should consider running in my place."

"*Me?*" CeeCee sounded disgusted. "First of all, I was not duly nominated. And second of all, I will never swing the male vote. I mean, let's face it, Suze. You're the one with the looks *and* the brains. You're like the Reese Witherspoon of our grade. I'm more like . . . Dick Cheney."

"CeeCee," I said, "you are way underestimating yourself. You—"

"You know what?" CeeCee sounded bitter. "Forget it. I don't care. I don't care what happens. Let Paul Look-at-My-New-BMW Slater be our class vice president. I give up."

She would have slammed the receiver down then, I could tell, if she'd been holding a normal phone. As it was, she could only hang up on me. I had to say hello a few more times, just to be sure, but when no one answered, I knew.

"Well," I said, hanging up. "She's mad."

"It sounded like it," Jesse said. "Who is this new person, the one running against you, who she is so afraid will win?"

And there it was. The direct question. The direct question, the truthful answer to which was, "Paul Slater." If I did not answer it that way—by saying "Paul Slater"—I would really and truly be lying to Jesse. Everything else I'd told him lately had been only half-truths, or maybe white lies.

But this one. This was the one that later, if he ever found out the truth, was going to get me in trouble.

I didn't know then, of course, that later was going to be three hours later. I just assumed later would be, you know, next week, at the earliest. Maybe even next month. By which point, I'd have thought up an appropriate solution to the Paul Slater problem.

But since I thought I had plenty of time to sort the whole thing out before Jesse got wind of it, I said, in response to his question, "Oh, just this new guy."

Which would have worked out fine if, a few hours later, David hadn't knocked on my bedroom door and went, "Suze? Something just came for you."

"Oh, come on in."

David threw open my door, but I couldn't see him. All I could see from where I lay on my bed was a giant bouquet of red roses. I mean, there had to have been two dozen at least.

"Whoa," I said, sitting up fast. Because even then, I had no clue. I thought Andy had sent them.

"Yeah," David said. I still couldn't see his face, because it was blocked by all the flowers. "Where should I put 'em?"

"Oh," I said with a glance at Jesse, who was staring at the flowers almost as astonishedly as I was. "Window seat is good."

David lowered the flowers—which had come complete with a vase—carefully onto my window seat, shoving a few of the cushions aside first to make a place for them. Then, once he'd gotten them stable, he straightened and said, plucking a small white tag from the green leaves, "Here's the card."

"Thanks," I said, tearing the tiny envelope open.

Get well soon! With love from Andy, was what I had expected it to say.

Or *We miss you, from the junior class of Junipero Serra Mission Academy*.

Or even, *You are a very foolish girl, from Father Dominic.*

What it said, instead, completely shocked me. The more so because of course Jesse was standing close enough to read over my shoulder. And even David, standing halfway across the room, could not have missed the bold, black script:

Forgive me, Suze. With love, Paul.

chapter *twelve*

So, basically, I was a dead woman.

Especially when David, who did not, of course, know that Jesse was standing right there—or that he is the man I happen to love with an all-consuming passion . . . at least when Paul Slater was not kissing me—went, "Is that from that Paul guy? I thought so. He was asking me all these questions about why you weren't in school today."

I couldn't even bring myself to look in Jesse's direction, I was so mortified.

"Um," I said. "Yeah."

"What does he want you to forgive him for?" David wanted to know. "The whole vice president thing?"

"Um," I said. "I don't know."

"Because you know, your campaign is really in trouble," David said. "No offense, but Kelly's handing out candy bars. You better come up with something gimmicky fast, or you might lose the election."

"Thanks, David," I said. "Bye, David."

David looked at me strangely for a moment, as if not sure why I was dismissing him so abruptly. Then he glanced around the room, as if realizing for the first time that we might not be alone, turned beet red, and said, "Okay, bye," and was out of my room like a shot.

Summoning all my courage, I turned my head toward Jesse and went, "Look, it's not what you . . ."

But my voice trailed off, because beside me, Jesse was looking murderous. I mean, really, like he wanted to murder someone.

Only it was anybody's guess who he wanted to murder, because I think at that point, I was as prime a candidate for assassination as Paul.

"Susannah," Jesse said in a voice I'd never heard him use before. "What is this?"

The truth was, Jesse had no right to be mad. No right at all. I mean, he'd had his chance, hadn't he? Had it, and blown it. He was just lucky I am not the kind of girl who gives up easily.

"Jesse," I said. "Look. I was going to tell you. I just forgot—"

"Tell me what?" The small scar through Jesse's right eyebrow—not the result, I had learned, of a knife fight with a bandito, as I had always rather romantically assumed, but from, of all things, a dog bite—was looking very white, a sure sign Jesse was very, very angry. As if I couldn't tell by the tone of his voice. "Paul Slater is back in Carmel, and you don't tell me?"

"He isn't going to try to exorcise you again, Jesse," I said hastily. "He knows he'd never get away with it, not while I'm around—"

"I don't care about that," Jesse said scornfully. "It's you he left for dead, remember? And this person is going to your school now? What does Father Dominic have to say about this?"

I took a deep breath. "Father Dominic thinks we should give him another chance. He—"

But Jesse didn't let me finish. He was up and off my bed, pacing the room and muttering under his breath in Spanish. I had no idea what he was saying, but it did not sound pleasant.

"Look, Jesse," I said. "This is exactly why I didn't tell you. I knew you were going to fly off the handle like this—"

"Fly off the handle?" Jesse threw me an incredulous look. "Susannah, he tried to kill you!"

I shook my head. It took a lot of guts, but I did it anyway.

"He says he didn't, Jesse," I said. "He says . . . Paul says I would have found my way out of there on my own. He says something about there being these people called shifters, and that I'm one of them. He says they're different from mediators, that instead of just being able to, you know, see and speak to the dead, shifters can move freely through the realm of the dead, as well. . . ."

But Jesse, instead of being impressed with this bit of news, only looked more angry.

"It sounds as if you and he have been doing a lot of talking lately," he said.

If I hadn't known better, I might have thought Jesse sounded almost . . . well, jealous. But since I knew good and well—as he had made it only too clear—that he did not feel about me the way that I feel about him, I simply shrugged.

"What am I supposed to do, Jesse? I mean, he goes to my school now. I can't just ignore him." I didn't, of course, have to go over to his house and French-kiss him, either. But that was one thing I was keeping from Jesse at all costs. "Besides, he seems to know stuff. Mediator stuff. Stuff Father

Dominic doesn't know, maybe hasn't ever even dreamed of. . . ."

"Oh, and I'm certain Slater is only too happy to share all he knows with you," Jesse said very sarcastically.

"Well, of course he is, Jesse," I said. "I mean, after all, we both have this sort of unusual gift. . . ."

"And he was always so eager to share information about that gift with the other mediators of his acquaintance," Jesse said.

I swallowed. Jesse had me there. Why was Paul so keen on mentoring me? Judging by the way he'd jumped me in his bedroom, I had a pretty good idea. Still, it was hard to believe his motives could be entirely lascivious. There were way prettier girls than me who went to the Mission Academy whom he could have had with a lot less trouble.

But none of them, I knew, shared our unique ability.

"Look," I said. "You're overreacting. Paul's a jerk, it's true, and I wouldn't trust him farther than I could throw him. But I really don't think he's out to get me. Or you."

Jesse laughed, but not like he really found anything amusing in the situation. "Oh, it's not me I think he's out to get, *querida*. I am not the one he's sending roses to."

I glanced at the roses. "Well," I said, feeling myself blush. "Yes. I can see your point. But I think he only sent those because he really does feel bad about what he did." I didn't mention Paul's most recent transgression against me, of course. I let Jesse think I meant the stuff Paul had pulled over the summer.

"I mean, he doesn't have anyone," I went on. "He really doesn't." I thought of the big glass house Paul lived in, of the spare and uncomfortable furniture in it. "I think . . . Jesse, I honestly think part of Paul's problem is that he's really, really lonely. And he doesn't know what to do about it, because no one ever taught him, you know, how to act like a decent human being."

Jesse wasn't having any of that, though. I could feel sorry for Paul all I wanted—and a part of me truly did, and I don't even mean the part that considered Paul a really excellent kisser—but to Jesse the guy was, is, and always would be dog meat.

"Well, for someone who doesn't know how to act like a decent human being," he said, going over to the roses and flicking one of the fat, scarlet buds, "he is certainly doing a good imitation of how one might behave. One who happens to be in love."

I felt myself turning as red as the roses Jesse was standing beside.

"Paul is not in love with me," I said. "Believe me." Because guys who were in love with girls did not send minions to try to keep them from fleeing the premises. Did they? "And even if he were, he sure isn't now. . . ."

"Oh, really?" Jesse nodded at the card in my hand. "I think his use of the word *love*—not *sincerely* or *cordially* or *truly yours*—would indicate otherwise, would it not? And what do you mean, if he were, he isn't now?" His dark-eyed gaze grew even more intense. "Susannah, did something . . . happen between the two of you? Something you aren't telling me?"

Damn! I looked down at my lap, letting some of my hair hide my face, so he couldn't see how deeply I was blushing.

"No," I said to the bedspread. "Of course not."

"Susannah."

When I looked up again, he was no longer standing by the roses. Instead, he was standing by the side of my bed. And he had lifted one of my hands in his own and was looking down at me with that dark, impenetrable gaze of his.

"Susannah," he said again. Now his voice was no longer murderous. Instead, it was gentle, gentle as his touch. "Listen to me. I'm not angry. Not with you. If there's something . . . anything . . .

you want to tell me, you can."

I shook my head, hard enough to cause my hair to whip my cheeks. "No," I said. "I told you. Nothing happened. Nothing at all."

But still Jesse didn't release my hand. Instead, he stroked the back of it with one calloused thumb.

I caught my breath. *Was this it?* I wondered. Was it possible that after all these weeks of avoiding me, Jesse was finally—*finally*—going to confess his true feelings for me?

But what, I thought, my heart drumming wildly, if they weren't the feelings I hoped? What if he didn't love me after all? What if that kiss had just been . . . I don't know. An experiment or something? A test I'd failed? What if Jesse had decided he just wanted to be friends?

I would die, that's all. Just lie down and die.

No, I told myself. No one clutched someone else's hand the way Jesse was clutching mine and told her that he *didn't* love her. No way. It wasn't possible. Jesse loved me. He *had* to. Only something—or someone—was keeping him from admitting it. . . .

I tried to encourage him into making the confession I so longed to hear.

"You know, Jesse," I said, not daring to look him in the eye but keeping my gaze on the fingers holding mine. "If there's anything *you* want to tell *me*, you can. I mean, feel free."

I swear he was about to say something. I *swear* it. I finally managed to lift my gaze to his, and I swear that when our eyes met, something passed between us. I don't know what, but *something*. Jesse's lips parted, and he was about to say who knows what, when the door to my room burst open. CeeCee, followed by Adam, came in, looking angry and carrying a whole lot of poster board.

"All right, Simon," CeeCee snarled. "Enough slacking. We need to get down to business, and we need to get down to business *now*. Kelly and Paul are whupping our butts. We have got to come up with a campaign slogan, and we have to come up with it now. We have one day until the election."

I blinked at CeeCee as astonishedly as Jesse was doing. He had dropped my hand as if it were on fire.

"Well, hi, CeeCee," I said. "Hi, Adam. Nice of you two to drop by. Ever heard of knocking?"

"Oh, please," CeeCee said. "Why? Because we might interrupt you and your precious Jesse?"

Jesse, upon hearing this, raised his eyebrows. Way up.

Blushing furiously—I mean, I didn't want him to know I'd been talking about him to my friends—I said, "CeeCee, shut up."

But CeeCee, who had dropped the poster board on the floor and was now scattering Magic Markers everywhere, went, "We knew he wasn't here. There's no car in the driveway. Besides, Brad said to go on up."

Of course he had.

Adam, spying the roses, whistled. "Those from him?" he wanted to know. "Jesse, I mean? Guy's got class, whoever he is."

I have no idea how Jesse reacted upon hearing this, since I didn't dare glance in his direction.

"Yes," I said, just to skip the complicated explanations. "Listen, you guys, this really isn't a very good—"

"Ew!" CeeCee, on the floor by the poster board, was finally in a position to get a good look at my feet for the first time. "That is disgusting! Your feet look just like the feet of those people they pulled down off Mount Everest. . . ."

"That was frostbite," Adam said, bending to scrutinize my soles. "Their feet were black. Suze's got the opposite problem, I think. Those are burn blisters."

"Yeah, they are," I agreed. "And they really

hurt. So if you don't mind—"

"Oh, no," CeeCee said. "You are not getting rid of us that easily, Simon. We need to come up with a campaign slogan. If I'm going to abuse my photocopying privileges in my capacity as editor of the school paper by running off hand flyers—don't worry, I already got a bunch of my sister's fifth grade classmates to agree to pass them out for us at lunch—I want to make sure they at least say something good. So. What should they say?"

I sat there like a lump, my mind completely filled with one thing and one thing only: Jesse.

"I'm telling you," Adam said, uncapping a Sharpie and taking a deep, long sniff of its tip. "Our slogan should be Vote Suze: She Doesn't Suck."

"Kelly," CeeCee said with some disdain, "would have a field day with that one. We'd be slapped with a defamation of character suit in no time for implying that Kelly sucks. Her dad's a lawyer, you know."

Adam, done sniffing the Sharpie, said, "How about Suze Rules?"

"That doesn't exactly rhyme," CeeCee pointed out. "Besides, then the implication is that the student government is a monarchy, which of course it is not."

I risked a glance at Jesse, just to see how he was taking all of this. He did not appear, however, to be paying much attention. He was staring at Paul's roses.

God, I thought. When I got back to school, I was so going to kill that guy.

"How about," I said, hoping to hurry CeeCee and Adam along so that I could have some privacy with my would-be boyfriend again, "Simon Says Vote for Suze."

CeeCee, kneeling beside the poster board, cocked her head at me, the sun, slanting into my west-facing windows, making her white-blond hair look bright yellow.

"'Simon Says Vote for Suze,'" she repeated, slowly. "Yeah. Yeah, I like that. Good one, Simon."

And then she bent down to start writing the slogan on the pieces of poster board scattered across my floor. It was clear that neither she nor Adam was going to be leaving anytime soon.

I glanced in Jesse's direction again, hoping to signal to him, as subtly as I could, how sorry I was for the interruption.

But Jesse, I saw, much to my dismay, had disappeared.

Wasn't that just like a guy? I mean, you finally get him to a point where he's apparently ready to make the big confession—whatever it was going to be—and then, *bam*. He disappears on you.

It's even worse when the guy happens to be dead. Because it wasn't even like I could have his license plate traced or whatever.

Not that I could blame him for leaving, I guess. I mean, I probably wouldn't have wanted to hang around in a room—that now smelled distinctly of Magic Marker—with a bunch of people who couldn't see me.

Still, I couldn't help wondering where he'd gone. I hoped to trail along after Neil Jankow, and keep me from having yet another ghost— Neil's brother Craig—to deal with. And when he'd be back.

It wasn't until I glanced at Paul's roses again that the really horrible part of it all occurred to me. And that was that the question wasn't *when* Jesse would be back. It was really *if*. Because of course, if you thought about it, why would the guy bother coming back at all?

I told CeeCee and Adam that I wasn't crying. I told them my eyes were watering from all the marker fumes. And they seemed to believe me.

Too bad the only person I didn't seem able to fool anymore was myself.

chapter *thirteen*

It didn't take me long to figure out where Jesse had disappeared to.

I mean, in the vast spectrum of things. Actually, it took me another day and a half. That's how long it was before the swelling in my feet went down, and I was able to squeeze my feet into a pair of Steve Madden slides and go back to school.

Where I was promptly called to the principal's office.

Seriously. It was part of Father Dom's morning announcements. He went, into the PA, "And let's all remember to remind our parents about the feast of Father Serra, which will take place here at the mission tomorrow starting at ten o'clock. There will be food and games and music and fun. Susannah Simon, after assembly, would you please come to the principal's office?"

Just like that.

I assumed Father Dom wanted to see how I was doing. You know, I had been out of school for two whole days, thanks to my feet. A nice person would naturally wonder if I was all right. A nice person would be concerned about my well-being.

And it turned out, Father D. was totally concerned about my well-being. But more spiritually than physically.

"Susannah," he said, when I walked through his office door—well, *walk* might be too strong a word for how I was getting around. I was still sort of hobbling. Fortunately, my slides were super cushioned, and the wide black band that held them to my feet completely covered most of the unsightly Band-Aids.

I still sort of felt like I was walking on mushrooms, though. Some of those blisters on the soles of my feet had gone hard as rocks.

"When," Father Dominic asked, "were you going to tell me about you and Jesse?"

I blinked at him. I was sitting in the visitor's chair across from his desk where I always sit while we have our little chats. As usual, I had fished a toy out from the good father's bottom drawer, where he keeps the juvenile parapher- nalia teachers confiscate from their pupils. Today I had hold of some Silly Putty.

"What about me and Jesse?" I asked blankly, because I genuinely had no idea what he was talking about. I mean, why would I ever suspect that Father Dom knew about me and Jesse . . . the truth about me and Jesse? I mean, who would ever have told him?

"That you . . . that you two . . . " Father Dom seemed to be having some trouble choosing his words.

That's how I got his meaning before he ever even got the whole sentence out.

"That you and Jesse are . . . I believe the term these days is *an item*," he finally blurted.

I immediately turned as red as the robes of the archbishop, who'd be descending upon our school at any moment.

"We—we aren't," I stammered. "An item, I mean. Actually, nothing could be further from the truth. I don't know how—"

And then, in a burst of intuition, I knew. I knew exactly how Father Dom had found out. Or thought I did, anyway.

"Did Paul tell you that?" I demanded. "Because I am really surprised at you, Father, for listening to a guy like that. Did you know that he is at least partly responsible for my blisters? I mean, he totally came on to me—" I didn't feel it was necessary, under the circumstances, to add that I hadn't resisted. At all. "And then when I tried to leave, he sicced this Hell's Angel after me—"

Father Dom interrupted me. Which is something Father Dominic does not do often.

"Jesse himself told me," he said. "And what is this about you and Paul?"

I was too busy gaping at him to pay attention to his question.

"*What?*" I exclaimed. "*Jesse* told you?" I felt as if the world as I knew it had suddenly been turned upside down, topsy-turvy, and inside out. Jesse had told Father Dom that we were an item? That he had feelings for me? Before he'd even bothered to tell me? This could not be happening. Not to me. Because incredibly good things like this never happened to me. Never.

"What, exactly," I asked carefully, because I wanted to make sure that, before I got my hopes up, I got the story straight, "did Jesse tell you, Father Dom?"

"That you kissed." Father Dominic said the

word so uncomfortably, you'd have thought there were tacks on the seat of his chair. "And I must say, Susannah, that I am disturbed that you said nothing of this to me the other day when we spoke. I have never been so disappointed in you. It makes me wonder what else you are keeping from me—"

"I didn't tell you," I said, "because it was just one lousy kiss. And it happened *weeks* ago. And since then, nothing. I mean it, Father D." I wondered if he could hear the frustration in my voice, and found that I didn't even care. "Not even nothing. A big *fat* nothing."

"I thought you and I were close enough that you would share something of this magnitude with me," Father Dominic said all glumly.

"Magnitude?" I echoed, smashing the Silly Putty in my fist. "Father D., what magnitude? Nothing happened, okay?" Much to my everlasting disappointment. "I mean, not what you're thinking, anyway."

"I realize that," Father Dominic said gravely. "Jesse is far too honorable a young man to have taken advantage of the situation. However, you must know, Susannah, that I cannot in good conscience allow this to continue—"

"Allow *what* to continue, Father D.?" I could

not believe I was even having this conversation. It was almost as if I had woken up in Bizarro World. "I told you, nothing—"

"I owe it to your parents," Father Dominic went on, as if I hadn't spoken, "to look out for your spiritual welfare as well as your physical well-being. And I have an obligation to Jesse, as well, as his confessor—"

"As his *what*?" I yelled, feeling as if I might fall out of my chair.

"There is no need to shout, Susannah. I believe that you heard me perfectly well." Father Dom looked about as miserable as I was just beginning to feel. "The fact is, that in light of . . . well, the current situation, I have advised Jesse that he needs to move into the rectory."

Now I did fall out of my chair. Well, I didn't fall out of it, exactly. I tumbled out of it. I tried to leap, but my feet were too sore for leaping. I settled for lunging at Father Dom. Except that there was this huge desk separating us, so I couldn't, as I wanted, grab big handfuls of his vestments and shriek *Why? Why?* in his face. Instead, I had to grip the edge of his desk very tightly and go, in the kind of shrill, girl voice I hate but couldn't stop emitting at that point, "The rectory? The *rectory*?"

"Yes, the rectory," Father Dominic said defensively. "He will be perfectly content there, Susannah. I know it will be difficult for him to adjust to spending his time somewhere other than—well, the place where he died. But we live very simply at the rectory. In many ways, it will be much like what Jesse was accustomed to when he was alive. . . ."

I was really having a lot of trouble processing what I was hearing.

"And Jesse *agreed* to this?" I heard myself asking in that same shrill, girl's voice. Whose voice *was* that, anyway? Surely not my own. "Jesse said he'd do it?"

Father Dominic looked at me in a manner I can only describe as pitying.

"He did," he said. "And I am more sorry than I can say that you had to find out this way. But perhaps Jesse felt . . . and I must say, I agree with . . . that such a scene might . . . well, a girl of your temperament might . . . well, you might have made it difficult. . . ."

And then, from out of nowhere, the tears came. My only warning was a sharp tingle in my nose. The next thing I knew, I was fighting back sobs.

Because I knew what Father Dom was trying to say. It was all there, in hideous black and white.

Jesse didn't love me. Jesse had never loved me. That kiss—that kiss had been an experiment after all. Worse than an experiment. A mistake, even. A horrible, miserable mistake.

And now Jesse knew that I'd lied to him about Paul—knew that I'd lied to him, and worse, probably guessed why I'd lied . . . that I love him, that I'd always loved him, and didn't want to lose him—he was moving out, rather than telling me the truth, that he didn't return my feelings. Moving out! He would rather have moved out than have spent another day with me! That's the kind of pathetic loser I am!

I fell back into the chair in front of Father Dom's desk, weeping. I didn't even care what Father Dom thought—you know, about me crying over a guy. It wasn't like I could just stop loving Jesse now that I knew—for absolute sure, once and for all—that he didn't love me back.

"I d-don't understand," I said, into my hands. "What . . . what did I do wrong?"

Father Dominic's voice sounded gently harassed. "Nothing, Susannah. You did nothing wrong. It's just better this way. Surely you can see that."

Father Dominic really isn't very good at dealing with love affairs. Ghosts, yes. Girls who've had their hearts stomped on? Not so much.

Still, he did his best. He actually got up from behind the desk, came around it, and laid one of his hands over my shoulder and patted it kind of awkwardly.

I was surprised. Father D. wasn't a real touchy-feely guy.

"There, there, Susannah," he said. "There, there. It will be all right."

Except that it wouldn't. It would never be all right.

But Father Dom wasn't finished.

"You two cannot go on as you have been. Jesse's got to leave. It's the only way."

I couldn't help letting out a humorless laugh at that one.

"The only way? To make him leave home?" I asked, angrily reaching up to wipe my eyes with the sleeve of my suede jacket. And you know what salt water does to suede. That's how far gone I was. "I don't think so."

"It isn't his home, Susannah," Father D. said kindly. "It's your home. It was never Jesse's home. It was the boardinghouse where he was murdered."

Hearing the word *murdered*, I am sorry to say, only made me cry harder. Father D. responded by patting my shoulder some more.

"Come now," he said. "You've got to be adult about this, Susannah."

I said something unintelligible. Even I didn't know what it was.

"I have no doubt that you will handle this situation, Susannah," Father Dom said, "as you've handled all the others in your life, with . . . well, if not grace, then aplomb. And now you had better go. First period is nearly over."

But I didn't go. I just sat there, occasionally letting out a pathetic sniffle as the tears continued to stream down my face. I was glad I'd worn waterproof mascara that morning.

But Father D., instead of taking pity on me, the way a man of the cloth is supposed to do, only looked at me a little suspiciously. "Susannah," he said, "I hope . . . I don't believe I have to . . . well, I feel obligated to warn you. . . . You are a very headstrong girl, and I do hope you will remember what I spoke to you about once before. You are not to use your, er, feminine wiles on Jesse. I meant it then, and I mean it now. If you must cry about this, get it over with here in my office. But do not cry to Jesse. Don't make this harder on him than it already is. Do you understand?"

I stamped a foot, then, but as pain shot up my

leg, instantly regretted the action.

"God," I said not very graciously. "What do you take me for? You think I'm going to beg him to stay or something? If he wants to go, that's fine by me. More than fine. I'm *glad* he's going." Then my voice caught on another traitorous sob. "But I just want you to know, it's not *fair*."

"Very little in life is fair, Susannah," Father Dominic said sympathetically. "But I shouldn't have to remind you that you have far, far more blessings in your life than many people. You are one very lucky girl."

"Lucky," I said with a bitter laugh. "Yeah, right."

Father Dominic looked at me. "You seem better now, Susannah," he said. "So perhaps you won't mind running along now. I have a lot of work to do concerning the feast tomorrow. . . ."

I thought about how much I hadn't told him. I mean, about Craig and Neil Jankow, not to mention Paul and Dr. Slaski and the shifters.

I should have told him about Paul. At the very least, I should have told him his whole fresh-start theory. Then again, maybe not. Paul was definitely up to no good, as my aching feet could attest.

But I was, I'll admit, a little bit peeved with Father Dominic. You would have thought he'd have shown me a little bit more compassion. I mean, he'd basically just broken my heart. Worse, he'd done it on Jesse's order. Jesse didn't even have the guts to tell me to my face that he didn't love me. No, he had to make his "confessor" do it. Nice one. Really made me sorry I'd missed out on life in the 1850s. Must have been sweet— everyone going around, making priests do their dirty work.

I couldn't, of course, run along, as Father Dom had suggested. I couldn't technically *run* any- where. But I hobbled out of his office, feeling extremely sorry for myself. I was still crying— enough so that when Father D.'s secretary saw me, she went, with motherly concern, "Oh, hon. You all right? Here, have a tissue," which was a lot more comforting than anything Father D. had done for me in the past half hour.

I took the tissue and blew my nose, then took a few more for the road. I had a feeling I was going to be bawling my eyes out until at least third period.

Stepping out into the breezeway along the courtyard, I tried to get a hold of myself. Okay. So the guy didn't like me. Lots of guys hadn't liked me in the past, and I'd never lost it like this. And, okay, this was *Jesse*, the person I loved best in all the world. But, hey, if he didn't want me back, that was just fine. You know what it was? Yeah, it was *his* loss, that's what it was.

So why couldn't I stop crying?

What was I going to do without him? I mean, I had totally gotten used to having Jesse around all the time. And what about his cat? Was Spike going to go live at the rectory, too? I guess he would have to. I mean, that ugly cat loved Jesse as much as I did. Lucky cat, getting to go live with Jesse.

I wandered along the length of the breezeway, looking out at the sun-soaked courtyard without really seeing it. *Maybe*, I thought, *Father D. was right*. Maybe it was better this way. I mean, let's say, just for a minute, that Jesse liked me back. Better than liked me. Loved me, even. Where was it going to go? It was like Paul had said. What were we going to do? Date? Go to the movies together? I would have to pay, and it would just be for one ticket. And if anyone saw me, to all appearances sitting by myself, I would look like the biggest dork in the world. How lame.

What I needed, I realized, was a real boyfriend. Not just a guy people besides me could see, either, but a guy I liked, who actually liked me back. That was what I needed. That was exactly what I needed.

Because when Jesse found out about it, it might make him realize what a colossal mistake he had just made.

It's kind of funny that as I was thinking this, Paul Slater suddenly leaped out at me from behind a column, and went, "Hey."

chapter *fourteen*

"Go away," I said.

Because the truth was, I was still sort of crying, and Paul Slater was just about the last person in the world I wanted to see me doing so. I was totally hoping he wouldn't notice.

No such luck. Paul went, "What's with the waterworks?"

"Nothing," I said, wiping my eyes with my jacket sleeve. I'd used up all the tissues Father Dom's secretary had given me. "Just allergies."

Paul reached out and jerked my hand away. "Here, use this."

And he passed me, of all things, a white handkerchief he'd pulled from his pocket.

Funny how, with everything else that was going on, all I could focus on was that white square of material. "You carry a *handkerchief*?" I asked in a voice that cracked.

Paul shrugged. "You never know when you might need to gag someone."

This was so not the answer I expected that I couldn't help laughing a little. I mean, Paul creeped me out a little . . . okay, a lot. But he could still be funny sometimes.

I mopped up my tears with the handkerchief, more conscious than I wanted to be of the proximity of its owner. Paul was looking particularly delectable that morning in a charcoal cashmere sweater and a chocolate-brown leather coat. I couldn't help looking at his mouth and remembering how it felt on mine. Which was good. More than good.

Then my gaze drifted toward his eye, the one I'd jabbed. No mark. The guy didn't bruise easily.

I wished the same could be said of me. Or of my heart, anyway.

I don't know if Paul noticed the direction of my gaze—I suppose it had been pretty obvious I'd been staring at his mouth. But all of a sudden, he lifted his arms and placed both hands against the three-foot-wide column I'd been leaning against—one of the columns that hold the roof of the breezeway up—sort of pinioning me in between them.

"So, Suze," he said in a friendly way. "What did Father Dominic want to see you about?"

Even though I was definitely in the market for a boyfriend, I wasn't so sure Paul was the guy for me. I mean, yeah, he was hot and all, and there was the whole mediator thing.

But there was also that whole thing where he'd tried to kill me. It's kind of hard just to let something like that go.

So I was sort of torn as I stood there, imprisoned between his arms. On the one hand, I wouldn't have minded reaching up and dragging his head down and laying a big fat one on his mouth.

On the other hand, giving him a good swift kick in the groin seemed equally appealing, given what he'd put me through the other day, what with the hot pavement and the Hell's Angel and all.

I didn't end up doing either. I just stood there, my heart beating kind of hard inside my chest. This was, after all, the guy about whom I'd been having nightmares for the past few weeks. That kind of thing doesn't go away just because the guy put his tongue in your mouth and you sort of liked it.

"Don't worry," I said in a voice that didn't sound at all like my own, it was so hoarse from all the crying. I cleared my throat, then said, "I didn't tell Father Dom anything about you, if that's what you're worried about."

Paul visibly relaxed as my words soaked in. He even lifted one of his hands away from the wall and fingered a coil of my hair that had been curled against my shoulder.

"I like your hair better down," he said approvingly. "You should always wear it down."

I rolled my eyes in order to hide the fact that my heart rate, when he touched me, sped up considerably, and I started to duck beneath the one arm he still had caging me in.

"Where do you think you're going?" he asked, moving to corner me once more, this time by taking a step closer, so that our faces were only about three inches apart. His breath, I was close enough to note, still smelled of whatever toothpaste he'd used that morning.

Jesse's breath never smells like anything, because, of course, he's not alive.

"Paul," I said in what I hoped was an even, completely toneless voice. "Really. Not here, okay?"

"Fine." He didn't move away, though. "Where, then?"

"Oh, God, Paul." I lifted a hand to my forehead. It felt hot. But I knew I didn't have a fever. Why was I so hot? It was cool in the breezeway. Was it Paul? Was it Paul who was making me feel this way? "I don't know, okay? Look, I have . . . I have a lot of stuff I have to figure out right now. Could you just . . . could you just leave me alone for a while, so I can think?"

"Sure," he said. "Did you get the flowers?"

"I got the flowers," I said. Whatever it was that was making me feel so feverish also forced me to add, even though I didn't want to, since all I wanted to do was run away and hide in the girls' room until it was time for classes to change, "But if you think I'm going to forget about what you did to me, just because you sent me a bunch of dumb flowers—"

"I said I was sorry, Suze," Paul said. "And I'm more sorry about your feet than I can say. You should have let me drive you home. I wouldn't have tried anything, I swear."

"Oh, yeah?" I looked up at him. He was a head taller than me, but his lips were still only inches from mine. I could meet them with my own without much of a problem. Not that I was going to. I didn't think. "What do you call what you're doing now?"

"Suze," he said, playing with my hair again. His breath tickled my cheek. "How else am I going to get you to talk to me? You've got this totally mistaken impression of me. You think I'm some kind of bad guy. And I'm not. I'm really not. I'm . . . well, I'm a lot like you, actually."

"Somehow, I seriously doubt that," I said. His proximity was making it difficult to talk. And not because he was scaring me. He still scared me, but in a different way now.

"It's true," he said. "I mean, we actually have a lot in common. Not just the mediator thing, either. I think our philosophy of life is the same. Well, except for the whole part where you want to help people. But that's just guilt. In every other way, you and I are identical. I mean, we're both cynical and mistrustful of others. Almost to the point of being misanthropic, I would go so far to say. We're old souls, Suze. We've both been around the block before. Nothing surprises us, and nothing impresses us. At least—" his ice-blue gaze bore into mine "—nothing until now. In my case, anyway."

"That may very well be, Paul," I said, as patronizingly as I was able—which wasn't very, I'm afraid, because his closeness was making it very difficult to breathe. "The only problem is, the person I mistrust most in the world? That'd be *you*."

"I don't know why," Paul said. "When we're clearly meant for each other. I mean, just because you met Jesse first—"

"*Don't*." The word burst from me like an explosion. I couldn't stand it. I couldn't stand hearing his name . . . not from those lips. "Paul, I'm warning you—"

Paul laid a single finger over my mouth.

"Shhh," he said. "Don't say things you'll only regret later."

"I am not going to regret saying this," I said, my lips moving against his finger. "You—"

"You don't mean it," Paul said confidently, sliding his finger from my mouth, over the curve of my chin, and down the side of my neck. "You're just scared. Scared to admit your true feelings. Scared to admit that I might know a few things you and wise old Gandalf, aka Father Dominic, might not. Scared to admit I might be right, and that you aren't as completely committed to your precious Jesse as you'd like to think. Come on, 'fess up. You felt something when I kissed you the other day. Don't deny it."

Felt something the other day? I was feeling something *now*, and all he was doing was running the tip of his finger down my neck. It wasn't right that this guy I hated—and I did hate him, I *did*—could make me feel this way . . .

. . . while the guy I loved could make me feel like such absolute—

Paul was leaning so close to me now, his chest brushed the front of my sweater.

"You want to try it again?" he asked. His mouth moved until it was only about an inch from mine. "A little experiment?"

I don't know why I didn't let him. Kiss me again, I mean. I wanted him to. There wasn't a nerve in my body that didn't want him to. After being dissed so hard back there in Father Dom's office, it would have been nice to know some-one—anyone—wanted me. Even a guy of whom I'd once been deathly afraid.

Maybe there was a part of me that still feared him. Or what he could do to me. Maybe that was what was making my heart beat so fast.

Whatever it was, I didn't let him kiss me. I couldn't. Not then. And not there. I craned my neck trying to keep my mouth out of his reach.

"Let's not," I said tensely. "I am having a very bad day, Paul. I would really appreciate it if you would *back off*—"

On the words *back off*, I laid both hands on his

chest and shoved him away from me as hard as I could.

Paul, not expecting this, staggered backward.

"Whoa," he said, when he'd regained his balance—and his composure. "What's the matter with you, anyway?"

"Nothing," I said, twisting his handkerchief in my fingers. "I just . . . I just got some bad news, is all."

"Oh, yeah?" This had clearly been the wrong thing to say to Paul, since now he looked positively intrigued, which meant he might never go away. "Like what? Rico Suave dump you?"

The sound that came out of me when he said that was a cross between a gasp and a sob. I don't know where it came from. It seemed to have been ripped from my chest by some unseen force. It startled Paul almost as much as it did me.

"Whoa," he said again, this time in a different tone. "Sorry. I . . . Did he? Did he really?"

I shook my head, not trusting myself to speak. I wished Paul would go away—shut up and go away. But he seemed incapable of doing either.

"I kind of thought," he said, "that there might be trouble in paradise when he never showed up to kick my ass after, you know, what happened at my house."

I managed to find my voice. It sounded ragged, but at least it worked. "I don't need Jesse," I said, "to fight my battles for me."

"You mean you didn't tell him," Paul said. "About you and me, I mean."

When I looked away, he said, "It has to be that. You didn't tell him. Unless you did tell him, and he just doesn't care. Is that it, Suze?"

"I have to get to class," I said, and turned around hastily to do just that.

Only Paul's voice stopped me.

"Question is, why didn't you tell him? Could it be because maybe, deep down, you're afraid to? Because maybe, deep down, you felt something . . . something you don't want to admit, even to yourself?"

I spun around.

"Or maybe," I said, "deep down, I didn't want a murder on my hands. Did you ever think about that, Paul? Because Jesse already doesn't like you very much. If I told him what you did to me—or tried to do to me, anyway—he'd kill you."

This was, as I knew only too well, a complete fabrication. But Paul didn't know that.

Still, he didn't take it the way I'd meant him to.

"See," Paul said with a grin. "You must like me a little, or you'd have gone ahead and let him."

I started to say something, realized the futility of it all, and spun around again to leave.

Only this time, classroom doors all around me were being flung open, and students started streaming out into the breezeway. There is no bell system at the Mission Academy—the trustees don't want to disturb the serenity of the courtyard or basilica by having a Klaxon ring every hour on the hour—so we just change classes every time the big hand reaches twelve. First period was, I realized, as the hordes started to mill around me, over.

"Well, Suze?" Paul asked, staying where he was, in spite of the sea of humanity darting past him. "Is that it? You don't want me dead. You want me around. Because you like me. Admit it."

I shook my head incredulously. It was, I realized, hopeless to argue with the guy. He was just too full of himself ever to listen to anyone else's point of view.

And then, of course, there was the little fact that he was right.

"Oh, Paul, there you are." Kelly Prescott came up to him, flinging her honey-blonde hair around. "I've been looking for you everywhere. Listen, I was thinking, about the voting, you know, at lunchtime. Why don't you and I stroll around the yard, passing out candy bars. You know, to remind people. To vote, I mean."

Paul wasn't paying any attention whatsoever to Kelly, though. His ice-blue gaze was still on me.

"Well, Suze?" he called, above the clanging of locker doors and the hum of conversation—though we were supposed to be quiet during period changes, so as not to disturb the tourists. "Are you going to admit it or not?"

"You," I said, shaking my head, "are in need of intensive psychotherapy."

Then I started to walk past them.

"Paul." Kelly was tugging on Paul's leather coat now, darting nervous glances at me the whole time. "Paul. Hello. Earth to Paul. The election. Remember? The election? This afternoon?"

Then Paul did something that would, I realized soon after, go down in the annals of the Mission Academy—and not just because CeeCee saw it, too, and filed it away for later reporting in the *Mission News*. No, Paul did something no one, with the possible exception of me, had ever done in the whole of the eleven years Kelly had been attending the school:

He dissed her.

"Why can't you," he said, pulling his coat out from beneath her fingers, "leave me alone for five freaking minutes?"

Kelly, as stunned as if he had slapped her, went, "Wh-what?"

"You heard me," Paul said. Though he did not seem to be aware of it, everyone in the breezeway had stopped what they were doing suddenly, just so they could watch what he'd do next. "I am freaking sick of you and this stupid election and this stupid school. Got me? Now get out of my sight, before I say something I might regret."

Kelly blinked as if her contact lens had slipped out. "Paul!" she said with a gasp. "But . . . but . . . the election . . . the candy bars . . ."

Paul just looked at her. "You can take your candy bars," he said, "and stick them up your—"

"Mr. Slater!" One of the novices, who are assigned to patrol the breezeway between classes to make sure none of us gets too noisy, pounced on Paul. "Get to the principal's office, this instant!"

Paul suggested something to the novice that I was quite sure was going to earn him a suspension, if not expulsion. It was so inflammatory, in fact, that even *I* blushed on his behalf, and *I* have three stepbrothers, two of whom use that kind of language regularly when their father isn't around.

The novice burst into tears and went running for Father Dominic. Paul looked after her fleeing, black-gowned little figure, then at Kelly, who was also crying. Then he looked at me.

There was a lot in that look. Anger, impatience, disgust.

But most of all—and I do not think I was mistaken about this—there was hurt. Seriously. Paul was hurt by what I'd said to him.

It had never occurred to me that Paul could be hurt.

Maybe what I had said to Jesse—about Paul being lonely—had been right after all. Maybe the guy really did just need a friend.

But he certainly wasn't making many at the Mission Academy, that was for sure.

A second later, he'd broken eye contact with me, turned around, and strode out of the school. Shortly after that, I heard the rev of the engine of his convertible and then the squeal of his tires on the asphalt of the parking lot.

And Paul was gone.

"Well," CeeCee said with no small amount of relish as she came up to me. "Guess that takes care of the election, doesn't it?"

Then she held up my wrist, prizefighter-style. "All hail Madam Vice President!"

chapter *fifteen*

Paul didn't come back to school that day.

Not that anybody expected him to. A sort of all-points bulletin went through the eleventh grade, stating that, if Paul did come back, he would be put on automatic suspension for a week. Debbie Mancuso heard it from a sixth grader who heard it from the secretary in Father Dom's office while she was there handing in a late pass.

It seemed the best thing that Paul stayed away until things cooled down a little. The novice he'd cursed at was rumored to have gone into hysterics, and had had to go lie down in the nurse's office with a cool compress across her forehead until she recovered. I had seen Father Dom looking grim faced, pacing around in front of the nurse's office door. I'd thought about going up to him and being all, "Told you so."

But it seemed too much like shooting fish in a barrel, so I stayed away.

Besides, I was still mad at him about the whole Jesse thing. The more I thought about it, the angrier I got. It was like the two of them had conspired against me. Like I was just a stupid sixteen-year-old girl with a crush they'd had to figure out some way to handle. Stupid Jesse was too scared even to tell me to my face he didn't like me. What did he think I was going to do, anyway? Pop him one in the face? Well, I sure felt like it now.

In between feeling like I just wanted to curl up somewhere and die.

I guess I wasn't alone in feeling that way. Kelly Prescott seemed to be feeling pretty bad, too. She handled her victimhood better than I did, though. She very dramatically tore the *Slater* part of the wrapper off all the candy bars she had left. Then she wrote *Simon* on the inside foil with a Sharpie instead. It appeared she and I were running mates once again.

I won the vice presidency of the Junipero Serra Mission Academy junior class unanimously, except for a single write-in vote for Brad Ackerman. Nobody wondered very much who could have voted for Brad. He hadn't even tried to disguise his handwriting.

Everyone forgave him, though, on account of the party he was throwing later that night. Guests had been instructed not to arrive until after ten, at which point it was determined that Jake, getting off his shift at Peninsula Pizza, would arrive with the keg and several dozen 'zas. Andy and my mom had left a note on the refrigerator that morning listing where they could be reached and forbidding us from having guests over while they were gone. Brad had found it particularly hilarious.

For my part, I had more important things to worry about than a stupid hot tub party.

Except that CeeCee and Adam wanted to go out after school to celebrate my victory—which really had turned out to be a hollow one, since my adversary had basically been kicked out of school. But Adam produced a bottle of sparkling cider for the occasion, and I couldn't say no to that, of course. He and CeeCee had both worked so hard on my campaign, to which I had contributed exactly nothing—well, except for a single slogan. I felt guilty enough that I rode with them to the beach after school, and stayed there long enough to toast the sunset, a custom dating back to the first time I'd won a student election, way back when I'd first moved to Carmel, nine months earlier.

When I got home, I discovered several things. One: Some of the guests had started arriving early, among them Debbie Mancuso, who had always had a bit of a crush on Brad, ever since the night I caught the two of them making out in the pool house at Kelly Prescott's. And two: She knew all about Jesse.

Or at least she thought she did.

"So who's this guy Brad says you're seeing, Suze?" she wanted to know, as she stood at the kitchen counter, artfully stacking plastic cups in preparation for the keg's arrival. Brad was outside with a couple of his cronies, giving the hot tub a heavy dose of chlorine, no doubt in anticipation of all the bacteria it was going to become filled with, once some of his more unsavory friends slid into it.

Debbie was in full-on party wear, which included a midriff-baring halter top and these balloony harem pants that I guess she thought hid the size of her butt, which was not small, but that really only made it look bigger. I don't like to be disparaging of members of my own sex, but Debbie Mancuso really was a bit of a parasite. She had been sucking Kelly dry for years. I just hoped she wouldn't turn her suckers on me next.

"Just a guy," I said coolly, moving past her to get a diet soda from the fridge. I was going to need a heavy-duty caffeine buzz, I knew, to fortify myself for the evening—first confronting Jesse, then the party.

"Does he go to RLS?" Debbie wanted to know.

"No," I said, cracking open the soda. Brad had, I saw, removed the note from Andy and my mom. Well, it was a little embarrassing, I guess. "He isn't in high school."

Debbie's eyes widened. She was impressed. "Really? He's in college, then? Does Jake know him?"

"No," I said.

When I did not elaborate, Debbie went, "That was really weird today, huh? About that Paul guy, I mean."

"Yeah," I said. I wondered whether or not Jesse was upstairs, waiting for me, or if he was just going to leave without saying good-bye. The way things had been going lately, I was betting on the latter.

"I kind of . . . I mean, some of the girls were

saying . . . " Debbie, never the most articulate of people, seemed to be having more trouble than usual spitting out what she wanted to say. "That that Paul guy seems to . . . like you."

"Yeah?" I smiled without warmth. "Well, at least someone does."

Then I drifted up the stairs to my room.

On my way up, I met David, coming down. He was carrying a sleeping bag, backpack, and the laptop he had won at computer camp for designing the most progressive video game. Max trailed on a leash behind him.

"Where are you going?" I asked him.

"Todd's house," he said. Todd was David's best friend. "He said Max and I could stay the night. I mean, it's not like anybody's going to be able to get any sleep around here tonight."

"A wise decision," I said approvingly.

"You should do the same thing," David suggested. "Stay over at CeeCee's."

"I would," I said, saluting him with my soda. "But I have a little business to attend to here."

David shrugged. "Okay. But don't say I didn't warn you."

Then he and Max continued down the stairs.

I was not surprised to find that Jesse was not in my room when I got there. Coward. I kicked off my slides, went into the bathroom, and locked the door. Not that locked doors make any difference to ghosts. And not that Jesse was going to show up anyway. I just felt more secure that way.

Then I ran a bath, undressed, and sank into it, letting the warm water caress my battered feet and soothe my tired body. Too bad there was nothing I could do to comfort my aching heart. Chocolate might have helped, maybe, but I didn't happen to have any in my bathroom.

The worst part of it all was that, deep down, I knew Father Dom was right about Jesse's moving out. It was better this way. I mean, what was the alternative? That he stayed here, and I just kept pining away for him? Unrequited love is all right in books and things, but in real life, it completely sucks.

It was just that—and this was the part that hurt the most—I could have sworn, all those weeks ago when he'd kissed me, that he'd felt something for me. Really. And I'm not talking about what I'd felt for Paul, which was, let's face it, lust. I'm warm for the guy's form, I'll admit it. But I don't love him.

I'd been so sure—so, so sure—that Jesse loved me.

But, obviously, I'd been wrong. Well, I was

wrong most of the time. So what else was new?

After I'd soaked for a while, I got out of the tub. I rebandaged my feet, then slid into my most comfortable, hole-filled jeans, the ones my mom told me I was never allowed to wear in public and was always threatening to throw away, coupled with a faded black silk T.

Then I walked back into my room, and found Jesse sitting in his usual place on the window seat, Spike on his lap.

He knew. I saw with a single glance that he knew Father Dom had talked to me and that he was just waiting—warily—to see what my reaction was going to be.

Not wanting to disappoint him, I said very politely, "Oh, you're still here? I thought you would have moved to the rectory by now."

"Susannah," he said. His voice was as low as Spike's got when he growled at Max through my bedroom door.

"Don't let me stop you," I said. "I hear there's going to be a lot of action over at the mission tonight. You know, getting ready for the big feast tomorrow. Lots of piñatas left to stuff, I hear. You should have a blast."

I heard the words coming out of my mouth, but I swear I don't know where they were coming from. I had told myself, back in the tub, that I was going to be mature and sensible about the whole thing. And here I was being peevish and childish, and it wasn't even a minute into the conversation.

"Susannah," Jesse said, standing up. "You must know it's better this way."

"Oh," I said with a shrug to show him how very, very unconcerned I was with the whole thing. "Sure. Give my regards to Sister Ernestine."

He just stood there, looking at me. I couldn't read his expression. If I'd ever been able to, I'd have known better than to have let myself fall in love with him. You know, on account of the whole his-not-loving-me-back thing. His eyes were dark—as dark as Paul's were light—and inscrutable.

"So that's all," he said, sounding, for reasons I couldn't begin to fathom, angry. "That's all you have to say to me?"

I couldn't believe it. He had some gall! Imagine, him being mad at *me*!

"Yes," I said. Then I remembered something. "Oh, no, wait."

The dark eyes flashed. "Yes?"

"Craig," I said. "I forgot about Craig. How is he doing?"

The dark eyes were hooded once again. Jesse seemed almost disappointed. As if *he* had anything to feel disappointed about! *I* was the one whose heart was being ripped out of her chest.

"He's the same," Jesse said. "Unhappy about being dead. If you want, I can have Father Dominic—"

"Oh," I said. "I think you and Father Dominic have done quite enough. I'll handle Craig, I think, on my own."

"Fine," Jesse said shortly.

"Fine," I said.

"Well. . . ." The dark-eyed gaze bore into mine. "Good-bye, Susannah."

"Yeah," I said. "See you around."

But Jesse didn't move. Instead, he did something I completely was not expecting. He reached one hand out and touched my face.

"Susannah," he said. His dark eyes—each one containing a tiny star of white where my bedroom light reflected off them—bore into mine. "Susannah, I—"

Only I never did find out what Jesse was going to say next, because the door to my bedroom suddenly swung open.

"Pardon me for interrupting," Paul Slater said.

chapter *sixteen*

Paul. I had forgotten all about him. Forgotten about him and just what, exactly, he and I had been up to these past few days.

Which was a lot of stuff I did not particularly want Jesse to know about.

"Knock much?" I asked Paul, hoping he would not notice the panic in my voice as Jesse and I pulled apart.

"Well," Paul said, looking pretty smug for a guy who'd been suspended from school that day. "I heard all the hilarity and figured you had guests. I didn't realize, of course, that you were entertaining Mr. De Silva."

Jesse, I saw, was meeting Paul's sardonic gaze

with a pretty hostile stare of his own. "Slater," Jesse said in a not particularly friendly voice.

"Jesse," Paul said pleasantly. "How are you this evening?"

"I was doing better," Jesse said, "before you got here."

Paul's dark eyebrows rose, as if he were surprised to hear this. "Really? Suze didn't tell you the news, then?"

"What n—" Jesse started to ask, but I interrupted quickly.

"About the shifting?" I actually stepped in front of Jesse, as if by doing so I could shield him from what I had a very bad feeling Paul was about to do. "And the soul transference thing? No, I haven't had a chance to tell Jesse about all that yet. But I will. Thanks for stopping by."

Paul just grinned at me. And something about that grin made my heart rate speed up all over again. . . .

And not because anyone was trying to kiss me, either.

"That's not why I'm here," Paul said, showing all of his very white teeth.

I felt Jesse tense beside me. Both he and Spike were behaving with extraordinary antagonism toward Paul. Spike had leaped onto the window-sill and, all his fur standing up, was growling at Paul pretty loudly. Jesse wasn't being quite that obvious about his contempt for the guy, but I figured it was only a matter of time.

"Well, if you're here for Brad's party," I said quickly, "you seem to be a little lost. It's downstairs, not up here."

"I'm not here for the party, either," Paul said. "I came by to return this to you." He dug into the pocket of his jeans and extracted something small and dark from it. "You left it in my bedroom the other day."

I looked down at what he held in his outstretched palm. It was my tortoiseshell hair clip, the one I'd been missing. But not since I'd been in his room. I'd been missing it since Monday morning, the first day of school. I must have dropped it then, and he'd picked it up.

Picked it up and held it all week, just so he could fling it in Jesse's face, as he was doing now.

And ruin my life. Because that's what Paul was. Not a mediator. Not a shifter. A ruiner.

A quick glance at Jesse showed me that those casually uttered words—*You left it in my bedroom the other day*—had hit home, all right. Jesse looked as if he'd been punched in the stomach.

I knew how he felt. Paul had that effect on people.

"Thanks," I said, snatching the hair clip from his hand. "But I dropped it at school, not your place."

"Are you sure?" Paul smiled at me. It was amazing how guileless he could look when he wanted to. "I could have sworn you left it in my bed."

The fist came out of nowhere. I swear I didn't see it coming. One minute I was standing there, wondering how in the world I was going to explain this one to Jesse, and the next thing I knew, Jesse's fist was plowing into Paul's face.

Paul hadn't seen it coming, either. Otherwise he would have ducked. Taken completely off guard, he went spinning right into my dressing table. Perfume and nail polish bottles rained down as Paul's body collided heavily with the ruffle-skirted desk.

"All right," I said, stepping quickly between them again. "Okay. Enough. Jesse, he's just trying to get a rise out of you. It was nothing, all right? I went over to his house because he said he knew some stuff about something called soul transference. I thought maybe it was something that might help you. But I swear, that's all it was. Nothing happened."

"Nothing happened," Paul said, his voice filled with amusement as he climbed to his feet. Blood was dripping from his nose all over the front of his shirt, but he didn't seem to notice. "Tell me something, *Jesse*. Does she sigh when you kiss her, too?"

I wanted to kill him myself. How could he? How *could* he?

The real question, of course, was how could *I*? How could I have been so stupid as to have let him kiss me like that? Because I *had* let him—I had even kissed him back. None of this would be happening if I had exercised a little more self-restraint.

I had been hurt, and I had been angry, and I had been, let's face it, lonely.

Just like Paul.

But I had never purposefully meant to hurt anyone.

This time Jesse's fist sent him spinning into the window seat, where Spike, not too happy about anything that was going on, let out a hiss and bounded out through the open window onto the porch roof. Paul landed facedown in the cushions. When he lifted his head, I saw blood all over the velvet throw pillows.

"That's *enough*," I said again, grabbing Jesse's arm as he pulled it back to land another blow. "God, Jesse, can't you see what he's doing? He's just trying to make you mad. Don't give him the satisfaction."

"That is not what I am trying to do," Paul said from the floor. He had rolled his head back against the blood-smeared cushion and was pinching the bridge of his nose to stem the tide of blood that was flowing more or less freely from it. "I am trying to point out to *Jesse* here that you need a real boyfriend. I mean, come *on*. How long do you think it's going to last? Suze, I didn't tell you before, but I'll tell you now because I know what you've been thinking. Soul transference only works if you toss out the soul that's currently occupying a body, then throw someone else's into it. In other words, it's *murder*. And I'm sorry, but you don't strike me as much of a murderer. Your boy Jesse's going to have to step into the light one of these days. You're just holding him back—"

I felt Jesse's arm move convulsively, and so I threw all my weight on it.

"Shut up, Paul," I said.

"And what about you, Jesse? I mean, what the hell can you give her?" Paul was laughing now, in spite of the blood that was still dripping from his face. "You can't even pay for her to have a damned cup of coffee—"

Jesse exploded from my grasp. That's the only way I can describe it. One minute he was there, and the next he was on top of Paul, and the two of them had their hands wrapped around each other's necks. They went crashing to the floor with enough force to jolt the entire house.

Not, I was certain, that anyone could hear them. Brad had turned on the stereo downstairs, and music was now pulsing up through the walls. Hip-hop—Brad's favorite. I was certain the neighbors were going to enjoy being lulled to sleep tonight by its dulcet tones.

On the floor, Jesse and Paul rolled around. I thought about smashing something over their heads. The thing is, they were both so hardheaded, it probably wouldn't do any good. Reasoning with them hadn't helped. I had to do something. They were going to kill each other, and it was all going to be my fault. My own stupid fault.

I don't know what put the idea of the fire extinguisher in my head. I was standing there, watching in dismay as Jesse sent Paul crashing very hard into my bookshelf, when suddenly I was just like, *Oh, yeah. The fire extinguisher.* I turned around and left my room, hurrying down the stairs, the pulse of the music getting louder and louder—and the sounds of the fight going on in my room growing farther away—with each step.

Downstairs, Brad's party was in full swing. Dozens of scantily clad, gyrating bodies crowded the living room, dancing to the beat. Half of them I didn't even recognize. Then I realized that was because they were Jake's friends from college. In my hurry I saw Neil Jankow holding on to one of those blue plastic cups Debbie Mancuso had been stacking so carefully on the kitchen counter. He sloshed foam everywhere as I tore past him.

So Jake, I knew now, had arrived with the keg.

I had to flatten myself against the wall just to make it past the people crammed in the hallway to the kitchen. Once I got there, I saw that it, too, was packed with people I had never seen before. A glance out the sliding glass doors revealed that the hot tub, which had been designed to hold a total of eight people, was currently holding close to thirty, most of whom were straddling one another. It was like my house had suddenly become the Playboy Mansion. I couldn't believe it.

I found the fire extinguisher under the sink, where Andy kept it in case of grease fires on the stove. I had to shout "excuse me" until I was hoarse before anybody would move enough to let me back out into the hallway. When I finally got there, I was shocked to hear someone screaming my name. I turned around, and there, to my utter astonishment, stood CeeCee and Adam.

"What are you doing here?" I yelled at them.

"We were invited," CeeCee yelled back—a little defensively, I noticed. I guessed that maybe the two of them had been getting some weird looks. They did not travel in the same social circle as my stepbrother Brad, by any means.

"Look," Adam said, holding up one of Brad's flyers. "We're legit."

"Well, great," I said. "Have fun. Listen, I have kind of a situation upstairs—"

"We'll come with you," CeeCee shouted. "It's too noisy down here."

It was not, I knew, going to be any quieter in my room. Plus there was the whole thing about Paul Slater fighting the ghost of my would-be boyfriend in there.

"Stay here," I told them. "I'll be back in a minute."

Adam, however, noticed the fire extinguisher and said, "Cool! Special effects!" and started after me.

There was nothing I could do. I mean, I had to

get back upstairs if I was going to keep Paul and Jesse from killing each other—or at least Jesse from killing Paul, since Jesse, of course, was already dead. CeeCee and Adam were going to have to deal with whatever they might see if they followed me.

I had hoped I might lose them on the stairs, but those hopes were dashed when, upon finally reaching the staircase, I saw Paul and Jesse tumbling down it.

That's what I saw, anyway. The two of them locked in a life-and-death struggle, rolling down the stairs on top of each other, each holding fistfuls of the other's clothing.

That's not what CeeCee and Adam—or anyone else who happened to be looking at that point—saw. What they saw was Paul Slater, bloody and bruised, falling down my stairs and seemingly hitting—well, himself.

"Oh, my God!" CeeCee cried, as Paul—she couldn't see that Jesse was there, too—crashed heavily at her feet. "Suze! What's going on?"

Jesse recovered himself before Paul did. He climbed to his feet, reached down, seized Paul by the arms, and pulled him up—just so he could hit him again.

That was not what CeeCee, Adam, and everyone else who happened to be looking in the direction of the stairs at that moment saw. What they saw was Paul jerked up by some unseen force and then thrown, by an invisible blow, across the room.

Much of the gyrating stopped. The music pounded on, but nobody was dancing anymore. Everybody was just standing there, staring at Paul.

"Oh, my God," CeeCee cried. "Is he on *drugs*?"

Adam shook his head. "It would explain a lot about that guy," he said.

Jake, meanwhile, apparently alerted by someone, pushed his way into the living room, took one look at Paul, writhing on the floor—with Jesse's hands around his neck, though I was the only one who could see this—and went, "Aw, Jesus."

Then, seeing me standing with the fire extinguisher in my hands, Jake strode over, took it away from me, and sent a jet of foamy white stuff spraying in Paul's direction.

It didn't do any good, really. All it did was cause the two of them to roll into the dining room—making a good many people jump out of the way—then crash into my mother's china cabinet—which of course teetered and fell, smashing all the plates inside.

Jake looked stunned. "What the hell is wrong with that guy? Is he wasted or what?"

Neil Jankow, who'd been standing nearby with his cup of beer still in his hand, said, "Maybe he's having a seizure. Somebody better call an ambulance."

Jake looked alarmed.

"No," he cried. "No, no cops! Nobody call the cops!"

At least, that's what he was saying right up until Jesse threw Paul through the sliding glass door to the deck.

It was the shower of glass that finally alerted all the people in the hot tub to the life-and-death battle that had been taking place inside. Screaming, they struggled to get out of the way of Paul's flailing body, only to find their escape dangerously impeded by shards of broken glass. Being barefooted, the people in the hot tub had nowhere to go as Paul and Jesse battered each other around the deck.

Brad, one of the people trapped in the hot tub—Debbie Mancuso hanging off him like a pilot fish—stared disbelievingly at the gaping hole where the sliding glass door had been. Then he thundered, "Slater! You are paying for a new door, you freak!"

Paul, however, wasn't in a position to be paying much attention. That's because he was struggling just to breathe. Jesse had him by the neck and was holding him over the side of the hot tub.

"Are you going to stay away from her?" Jesse demanded, as the lights from the Jacuzzi bottom cast them in an eery blue glow.

Paul gurgled, "No way."

Jesse dunked Paul's head beneath the water and held it there.

Neil, who'd followed Jake out onto the deck, pointed and cried, "Now he's trying to drown himself! Ackerman, you better do something, and quick."

"Jesse," I cried. "Let him go. It's not worth it."

CeeCee looked around. "Jesse?" she echoed confusedly. "He's here?"

Jesse was distracted enough that he loosened his hold somewhat, and Jake, with Neil's help, was able to pull Paul up, gasping for air, with blood now mingling with chlorinated water all down his shirt front.

I couldn't take it anymore. "You have to stop it," I said to Jesse and Paul. "That's enough. You've wrecked my house. You've made a mess of each other. And—" I added this last as I looked around and saw all the curious, half-frightened gazes aimed at me "—I think you've pretty much destroyed what little good reputation I once had."

Before either Jesse or Paul could reply, however, another voice broke in.

"I can't believe," Craig Jankow said, materializing to the left of his brother, "that you guys had a kegger, and no one invited me. Seriously," Craig continued, as I threw him an incredulous look, "this is some good stuff. You mediators really know how to throw a party."

Jesse wasn't paying any attention to the latecomer, however. He said to Paul, "Don't come near her again. Do you understand?"

"Eat me," Paul suggested.

Back he went into the hot tub with a splash. Jesse ripped him right out of Jake's grip.

The surprise was, this time Neil went under with Paul. That's because Craig, a quick learner, had decided to go ahead and follow through with his whole if-I'm-dead-my-brother-should-be-too thing, now that Jesse had shown him how.

"Neil!" Jake cried, trying to pull both Paul and his friend—who, as far as he knew, had inexplicably plunged into the hot tub face first—up from the bottom of the Jacuzzi. What he didn't know, of course, was that ghostly hands were holding both of them down.

I knew it, though. I also knew that there wasn't anything any of us could do to get them to let go. Ghosts have superhuman strength. There was no way any of us were going to get those two to give up their victims. Not until they were as dead as : . . well, as their killers.

Which was why I knew I was going to have to do something I really didn't want to do. I just didn't see any way out of it. Threats hadn't worked. Brute force hadn't worked. There was only one way.

But I really, really didn't want to take it. My chest was tight with fear. I could hardly breathe, I was so scared. I mean, the last time I'd been to that place, I'd nearly died. And I had no way of knowing whether or not Paul had told me the truth. What if I tried what he'd said, and I ended up somewhere even worse than where I'd ended up before?

Although it would be hard to imagine any place worse.

Still, what choice did I have? None.

I just really, really didn't want to take it.

But I guess we don't always get what we want.

My heart in my throat, I thrust my hands into the hot, churning water, and grabbed twin handfuls of shirt. I didn't even know whose clothes I had hold of. All I knew was, this was the only way

chapter *seventeen*

I wasn't alone. Paul was with me. And Craig Jankow, too.

"What the . . . ?" Craig looked up and down the long dark hallway, as eerily silent as Brad's party had been loud. "Where the hell are we?"

"Where you should have gone a long time ago," Paul said, carefully brushing lint off his shirt—though, since this was an alternative plane, and only his consciousness, not his actual body, was on it, there was no lint to brush. To me, Paul said with a smile, "Nice work, Suze. And on your first try, too."

"Shut up." I was in no mood for pleasantries. I was somewhere I really, really didn't want to be . . . a place that, every time I returned to in my nightmares, left me feeling completely physically and emotionally drained. A place that sucked the life out of me . . . not to mention my courage. "I'm not exactly happy about this."

"I can tell." Paul reached up and felt his nose. Since we were in the spirit world, and not the actual one, it was no longer bleeding. His clothes weren't wet, either. "You know the fact that we're up here means that our bodies, down there, are unconscious."

"I know," I said, glancing nervously up and down the long, fog-enshrouded hallway. Just like in my dreams, I couldn't see what was at either end. It was just a line of doors that seemed to go on forever.

"Well," Paul said, "that should get Jesse's attention, anyway. Your suddenly dropping off into a coma, I mean."

"Shut up," I said again. I felt like crying. I really did. And I hate crying. Almost more than I hate falling into bottomless pits. "This is all your fault. You shouldn't have antagonized him."

"And you," Paul said with a spark of anger, "shouldn't go around kissing—"

"Excuse me," Craig interrupted. "But could somebody maybe tell me exactly what—"

"Shut up," Paul and I said to him, at the exact same time.

Then, to Paul, I said, a catch in my voice, "Look, I'm sorry about what happened at your house. Okay? I lost my head. But that doesn't mean that there is anything going on between us."

"You lost your head," Paul repeated tonelessly.

"That's right," I said. The hairs on the back of my neck were standing up. I did not like this place. I didn't like the white plumes of fog that were licking my legs. I didn't like the tomblike stillness. And I especially didn't like that I couldn't see more than a few feet in front of me. Who knew where the floor might drop off from underneath?

"What if I want there to be something between us?" he asked.

"Too bad," I said, shortly.

He glanced over at Craig, who was beginning to wander down the hall, regarding the closed doors on either side of him with interest.

"What about shifting?" Paul asked.

"What *about* it?"

"I told you how to do it, didn't I? Well, there's other stuff I can show you. Stuff you've never even dreamed you could do."

I blinked at him. I thought back to what he'd

said that afternoon in his bedroom, about soul transference. There was a part of me that wanted to know what that was all about. There was a part of me that wanted to know about this very, very badly.

But there was an equally big part of me that wanted nothing whatsoever to do with Paul Slater.

"Come on, Suze," Paul went on. "You know you're dying to know. All your life you've been wondering who—or what—you really are. And I'm telling you, I have the answers. I *know*. And I'll teach you, if you'll let me."

I narrowed my eyes at him. "And what do *you* get out of this magnanimous offer of yours?" I wanted to know.

"The pleasure of your company," he said with a smile.

He said it casually, but I knew there was nothing casual about it at all. Which was why, in spite of how much I was dying to find out more about all the other stuff he claimed to know, I was reluctant to accept his offer. Because there was a catch. And the catch was that I was going to have to spend time with Paul Slater.

But it might be worth it. Almost. And not because I'd finally be getting some insight into the true nature of our so-called gift, but because I might, at last, be able to guarantee Jesse's safety . . . at least where Paul was concerned.

"Okay," I said.

To say Paul looked surprised would have been the understatement of the year. But before he could say anything, I added, gruffly, "But Jesse is off-limits to you. I really mean it. No more insults. No more fights. And no more exorcisms."

One of Paul's dark eyebrows went up. "So that's how it is," he said slowly.

"Yes," I said. "That's how it is."

He didn't say anything for so long that I figured he wanted to forget the whole thing. Which would have been fine by me. Sort of. Except for the Jesse part.

But then Paul shrugged and went, "Fine by me."

I stared at him, hardly daring to believe my own ears. Had I just engineered—at great personal sacrifice, it had to be admitted—Jesse's reprieve?

It was Paul's nonchalance about the whole thing that convinced me I had. Especially his response to Craig, when the latter reached out and rattled one of the doorknobs and called, "Hey, what's behind these doors?"

"Your just rewards," Paul said with a smirk.

Craig looked over his shoulder at Paul. "Really? My just rewards?"

"Sure," Paul said.

"Don't listen to him, Craig," I said. "He doesn't know what's behind those doors. It could be your just rewards. Or it could just be your next life. No one knows. No one has ever come out through one of them. You can only go in."

Craig looked speculatively at the door in front of him.

"Next life, huh?" he said.

"Or eternal salvation," Paul said. "Or, depending on how bad you've been, eternal damnation. Go on. Open it and find out whether you were naughty or nice."

Craig shrugged but he didn't take his eyes off the door in front of him.

"Well," he said. "It's gotta be better than hanging around down there. Tell Neil I'm sorry I acted like such a . . . you know. It's just that, well, it's just that it really wasn't very fair."

Then, laying a hand on the doorknob in front of him, he turned the handle. The door opened a fraction of an inch . . .

And Craig disappeared in a flash of light so blinding, I had to throw up my hands to protect my eyes.

"Well," I heard Paul saying, a few seconds later, "now that he's out of the way . . ."

I lowered my arms. Craig was gone. There was nothing left where he'd been standing. Even the fog looked undisturbed.

"Now can we get out of here?" Paul heaved a little shudder. "This place gives me the heebie-jeebies."

I tried to hide my astonishment that Paul felt exactly the way I did about the spirit plane. I wondered if he had nightmares about it, too. Somehow, I didn't think so.

But I didn't think I'd be having any more of them, either.

"Okay," I said. "Only . . . only how do we get back?"

"Same thing," Paul said, closing his eyes. "Just picture it."

I closed my eyes, feeling the warmth of Paul's fingers inside my arm, and the cool lick of the fog on my legs . . .

A second later, the awful silence was gone, replaced instead by the sounds of loud music. And screaming. And sirens.

I opened my eyes.

The first thing I saw was Jesse's face, hanging over mine. It looked pale in the flashing red and white lights of the ambulance that had pulled up alongside the deck. Beside Jesse's face was CeeCee's, and beside hers, Jake's.

CeeCee was the first one to go, "She's awake! Oh, my God, Suze! You're awake! Are you okay?"

I sat up groggily. I did not feel very good. In fact, I felt a little as if someone had hit me. Hard. I clutched my temples. Headache. Pounding headache. Nausea-inducing headache.

"Susannah." Jesse's arm was around me. His voice, in my ear, was urgent. "Susannah, what happened? Are you all right? Where . . . where did you go? Where's Craig?"

"Where he belongs," I said, wincing as red and white lights caused my headache to feel a thousand times worse. "Is Neil . . . is Neil all right?"

"He's fine. Susannah." Jesse looked about as shaky as I felt . . . which was pretty shaky. I didn't imagine that the past few minutes had been all that great for him. I mean, what with me being slumped over, unconscious, and for no apparent reason and all. My jeans were wet from where I'd landed in water from the hot tub. I could only imagine what my hair looked like. I feared passing a mirror.

"Susannah." Jesse's grasp on me was possessive. Delightfully so. "What happened?"

"Who's Neil?" CeeCee wanted to know. She glanced worriedly at Adam. "Oh, my God. She's delusional."

"I'll tell you later," I said, with a glance at CeeCee. A few feet away, I could see that Paul, too, was sitting up. Unlike Neil, over where the sliding glass door used to be, he was doing so without the aid of an EMT. But like Neil, Paul was coughing up plenty of chlorinated water. And not just his jeans were wet. He was soaked from head to toe. And his nose was bleeding profusely.

"What've we got here?" An EMT knelt down beside me, and, lifting my wrist, began to take my pulse.

"She passed out cold," CeeCee said officiously. "And no, she hadn't had anything to drink."

"Lotta that going around here," the EMT said. She checked my pupils. "You hit your head, too?"

"Not that I know of," I said, narrowing my eyes against the annoying glare of her little penlight.

"She might've," CeeCee said, "when she passed out."

The EMT looked disapproving. "When are you kids going to learn? Alcohol," she said severely, "and hot tubs do not mix."

I didn't bother to argue that I hadn't been drinking. Or, for that matter, sitting in the hot tub. I was, after all, fully dressed. It was enough that the EMT let me go after telling me that my vitals checked out and that I was to drink plenty of water and get some sleep. Neil, too, was given a clean bill of health. I saw him a little while later, calling for a cab on his cell phone. I went up to him and told him that it was safe to use his car now. He just looked at me like I was crazy.

Paul wasn't as lucky as Neil and me. His nose turned out to be broken, so they trundled him off to the ER. I saw him moments before they wheeled him away, and he did not look happy. He peered at me around the splint they'd taped to his face.

"Headache?" Paul asked in a phlegmy voice.

"A killer one," I said.

"Forgot to warn you," he said. "It always happens, post shifting."

Paul grimaced. I realized he was trying to smile. "I'll be back," he said in a pretty sad imitation of the Terminator. Then the EMTs returned to cart him away.

After Paul was gone, I looked around for Jesse. I had no idea what I was going to say to him . . . maybe something along the lines of how he wasn't going to have to worry about Paul anymore?

Only it ended up not mattering anyway, because

I didn't see him anywhere. Instead, all I saw was Brad, panting heavily, and coming my way.

"Suze," he cried. "Come on. Some idiot called the cops. We've got to hide the keg before they get here."

I just blinked at him. "No way," I said.

"Suze." Brad looked panicky. "Come on! They'll confiscate it! Or worse, arrest everybody."

I looked around and found CeeCee standing over by Adam's car. I called, "Hey, Cee. Can I come over and spend the night at your house?"

CeeCee called back, "Sure. If you'll tell me everything there is to know about this Jesse guy."

"Nothing to tell," I said. Because there really wasn't. Jesse was gone. And I had a pretty good idea where he'd gone, too.

And there wasn't a thing I could do about it.

chapter *eighteen*

"Face it, Suze," CeeCee said as she wolfed down her half of a cannoli we were sharing the next day at the feast of Father Serra. "Men suck."

"You're telling me," I said.

"I mean it. Either you want them and they don't want you, or they want you and you don't want them—"

"Welcome to my world," I said, glumly.

"Aw, come on," she said, looking taken aback by my tone. "It can't be *that* bad."

I wasn't in any sort of mood to argue with her. For one thing, I had only just, a little less than twelve hours later, gotten over my postshifting headache. For another, there was the little matter of Jesse. I wasn't all that keen to discuss the latest developments there.

It wasn't like I didn't have enough problems. Like, for instance, my mom and stepdad. They hadn't been *too* homicidal when they'd gotten home from San Francisco and discovered the shambles that had once been their home . . . not to mention the police summons. Brad was only grounded for life, and Jake, for going along with the whole party scheme—not to mention providing the alcohol—had his Camaro fund completely confiscated to pay whatever fines the party ended up costing. Only the fact that David had been safely at Todd's the whole time kept Andy from actually killing either of his two elder sons. But you could tell he was totally thinking about it anyway . . . especially after my mom saw what had happened to the china cabinet.

Not that either Andy or my mom was particularly happy with me, either—not because they knew the busted-up china cabinet was my fault, but for not ratting my stepbrothers out in the first place. I would have intimated that blackmail had been employed, but then they would have known that Brad had something on me that was worthy of blackmail.

So I kept my mouth shut, glad that for once, I

was more or less guiltless. Well, except where the china cabinet was concerned—though happily, no one but me knew it. Still, I knew I couldn't shirk my culpability there. I pretty much knew where any future babysitting earnings were going to go.

I am pretty sure they were thinking about grounding me, too. But the feast of Father Serra they could not keep me away from, on account of how, being a member of the student government, I was expected by Sister Ernestine to man a booth there. Which was how I'd ended up at the cannoli stand with CeeCee, who, as editor of the school paper, was also required to put in an appearance. After the preceding evening's activities—you know, massive brawl, trip to the netherworld, and then all-night gabfest accompanied by copious amounts of popcorn and chocolate—we were neither of us at our best. But the surprising number of attendees who plunked down a buck per cannoli didn't seem to notice the circles under our eyes . . . perhaps because we were wearing sunglasses.

"Okay," CeeCee said. It had been pretty dim of Sister Ernestine to put CeeCee and me in charge of a dessert booth, since most of the pastries we were supposed to be selling were disappearing down our throats. After a night like the one we'd had, we felt like we needed the sugar. "Paul Slater."

"What about him?"

"He likes you."

"I guess," I said.

"That's it? You *guess*?"

"I told you," I said. "I like someone else."

"Right," CeeCee said. "Jesse."

"Right," I said. "Jesse."

"Who doesn't like you back?"

"Well . . . yeah."

CeeCee and I sat in silence for a minute. All around us, mariachi music was playing. Over by the fountain, kids were batting at piñatas. The statue of Junipero Serra had been adorned with flowered leis. There was a sausage and peppers stand right alongside the taco stand. There were as many Italians in the church community as there were Latinos.

Suddenly, CeeCee, gazing at me from behind the dark lenses of her sunglasses, went, "Jesse's a ghost, isn't he?"

I choked on the cannoli I was scarfing down.

"Wh-what?" I asked, gagging.

"He's a ghost," CeeCee said. "You don't have to bother denying it. I was there last night, Suze. I saw . . . well, I saw stuff that can't be explained any other way. You were talking to him, but there wasn't anyone there. And yet someone was holding Paul's head under that water."

I went, feeling myself turn beet red, "You're nuts."

"No," CeeCee said. "I'm not. I wish I were. You know I hate stuff like that. Stuff that can't be explained scientifically. And those stupid people on TV, who claim they can speak to the dead. But—" A tourist came up, drunk on the bright sunshine, the fresh sea air, and the extremely weak beer they were serving over at the German booth. He put down a dollar. CeeCee handed him a cannoli. He asked for a napkin. We noticed that the napkin dispenser was empty. CeeCee apologized. The tourist laughed good-naturedly, took his cannoli, and went away.

"But what?" I asked nervously.

"But where you're concerned, I'm willing to believe. And some day," she added, picking up the empty napkin dispenser, "you are going to explain it all to me."

"CeeCee," I said, feeling my heart start to return to its normal rhythm. "Believe me. You're better off not knowing."

"No," CeeCee said, shaking her head. "I'm not.

I hate not knowing things." Then she shook the empty dispenser. "I'm going to go get a refill. You okay on your own for a minute?"

I nodded, and she went away. I don't know if she had any idea how badly she'd shaken me. I sat there, wondering what I ought to do. Only one other living person knew my secret—one other person besides Father Dom and Paul, of course—and even she, my best friend, Gina, back in Brooklyn, didn't know all of it. I had never told anyone else because . . . well, because who would believe it?

But CeeCee believed it. CeeCee had figured it out for herself, and she believed it. *Maybe*, I thought. Maybe it wasn't as crazy as I'd always thought.

I was sitting there, trembling, even though it was seventy-five degrees and sunny out. I was so deeply absorbed in my thoughts, I didn't hear the voice that was addressing me from the other side of the booth until he'd said my name—or a semblance of it, anyway—three times.

I looked up, and saw a young man in a pale blue uniform grinning at me. "Susan, right?" he said.

I looked from him to the face of the old man whose wheelchair he was pushing. It was Paul

Slater's grandfather and his attendant. I shook myself and stood up.

"Um," I said. "Hi." To say I was feeling a bit confused would have been the understatement of the year. "What are you—what are you doing here? I thought . . . I thought . . ."

"You thought he was housebound?" the nurse asked with a grin. "Not quite. No, Mr. Slater likes to get out. Don't you, Mr. Slater? In fact, he insisted on coming down here today. I didn't think it was appropriate, you know, given what happened to his grandson last night, but Paul's at home, recuperating nicely, and Mr. S. was adamant. Weren't you, Mr. S.?"

Paul's grandfather did something that surprised me then. He looked up at the nurse and said in a voice that was perfectly lucid, "Go and get me a beer."

The nurse frowned down at him. "Now, Mr. S.," he said. "You know your doctor says—"

"Just do it," Mr. Slater said.

The nurse, with an amused glance at me as if to say *Well, what are you going to do?* went off to the beer booth, leaving Mr. Slater alone with me.

I stared at him. The last time I had seen him, he'd been drooling. He wasn't drooling now. His blue eyes were rheumy, it was true. But I had a feeling they saw a lot more that was going on around him besides just *Family Feud* reruns.

In fact, I was sure of it, when he said, "Listen to me. We don't have much time. I was hoping you'd be here."

He spoke rapidly and softly. In fact, I had to lean forward, over the cannolis, to hear him. But though his voice was low, his enunciation was crystal clear.

"You're one of them," he said. "One of those shifters. Believe me, I know. I'm one, too."

I blinked at him. "You—you are?"

"Yes," he said. "And the name's Slaski, not Slater. Fool son of mine changed it. Didn't want people to know he was related to an old quack who went around talking about people with the ability to walk among the dead."

I just stared at him. I didn't know what to say. What *could* I say? I was more astonished by this than by what CeeCee had revealed.

"I know what my grandson told you," Mr. Slater—Dr. Slaski—went on. "Don't listen to him. He's got it all wrong. Sure, you have the ability. But it'll kill you. Maybe not right away but eventually." He stared out at me from a gray, liver-spotted mask of wrinkles. "I know what I'm talking about. Like that fool grandson of mine, I thought I was a god. No, I thought I *was* God."

I blinked at him. "But—"

"Don't make my mistake, Susan. You stay away from it. Stay away from the shadow world."

"But—"

But Paul's grandfather had seen his nurse coming back, and he quickly lapsed back into his semicatatonic state, and would say no more.

"Here you go, Mr. Slater," the nurse said, carefully holding the plastic cup to the old man's lips. "Nice and cold."

Dr. Slaski, to my complete disbelief, let the beer dribble down his chin and all over his shirt.

"Oops," the attendant said. "Sorry about that. Well, we'd better go get cleaned up." He winked at me. "Nice seeing you again, Susan. See you later."

Then he wheeled Dr. Slaski away, toward the duck-shooting booth.

And that, as far as I was concerned, was it. I had to get out. I could not take it a minute longer in the cannoli booth. I had no idea where CeeCee had disappeared to, but she was just going to have to deal with the pastry sales on her own for a while. I needed some quiet.

I slipped out from behind the booth and strode blindly through the crowds packing the courtyard, darting through the first open door I came across.

I found myself in the mission's cemetery. I didn't turn back. Cemeteries don't creep me out that much. I mean, though it might come as a surprise to learn, ghosts hardly ever hang out there. Near their graves, I mean. They tend to concentrate much more on the places they hung out while they were living. Cemeteries can actually be very restful, to a mediator.

Or a shifter. Or whatever it is that Paul Slater is convinced I am.

Paul Slater, who, I was beginning to realize, wasn't just a manipulative eleventh grader who happened to be warm for my form. No, according to his own grandfather, Paul Slater was . . . well, the devil.

And I had just sold my soul to him.

This was not information I could process lightly. I needed time to think, time to figure out what I was going to do next.

I stepped into the cool, shady graveyard, and turned down a narrow pathway that, by this point, had actually become sort of familiar to me. I went down it a lot. In fact sometimes, when I borrowed the hall pass, pretending I needed to visit the ladies' room during class, this was where

I went instead, to the mission cemetery and down this very path. Because at the end of it lay something very important to me. Something I cared about.

But this time, when I got to the end of the little stone path, I found that I was not alone. Jesse stood there, looking down at his own headstone.

I knew the words he was reading by heart, because I was the one who, with Father Dom, had supervised their carving.

HERE LIES HECTOR "JESSE" DE SILVA, 1830–1850, BELOVED BROTHER, SON, AND FRIEND.

Jesse looked up as I came to stand beside him. Wordlessly, he held his hand out over the top of the headstone. I slipped my fingers into his.

"I'm sorry," he said, his gaze darkly opaque as ever, "about everything."

I shrugged, keeping my gaze on the earth surrounding his headstone—dark as his eyes. "I understand, I guess." Even though I didn't. "I mean, you can't help it if you . . . well, don't feel the same way about me as I do about you."

I don't know what made me say it. The minute the words were out of my mouth, I wished the grave beneath us would open up and swallow me, too.

So you can imagine my surprise when Jesse

demanded, in a voice I barely recognized as his, it was so filled with pent-up emotion, "Is that what you think? That I *wanted* to leave?"

"Didn't you?" I stared at him, completely dumbstruck. I was trying very hard to remain coolly detached from the whole thing, on account of having had my pride stomped on. Still, my heart, which I could have sworn had shriveled up and blown away a day or two ago, suddenly came shuddering back to life, even though I warned it firmly not to.

"How could I stay?" Jesse wanted to know. "After what happened between us, Susannah, how could I stay?"

I genuinely had no idea what he was talking about. "What happened between us? What do you mean?"

"That kiss." He let go of my hand, so suddenly that I stumbled.

But I didn't care. I didn't care because I was beginning to think something wonderful was happening. Something glorious. I thought it all the more when I saw Jesse lift a hand to run his fingers through his hair, and I saw that they were shaking. His fingers, I mean. Why would his fingers be shaking like that?

"How could I stay?" Jesse wanted to know.

"Father Dominic was right. You need to be with someone your family and your friends can actually *see*. You need to be with someone who can grow old with you. You need to be with someone *alive*."

Suddenly, it was all beginning to make sense. Those weeks of awkward silences between us. Jesse's standoffishness. It wasn't because he didn't love me. It wasn't because he didn't love me, at all.

I shook my head. My blood, which I'd begun to suspect had somehow frozen in my veins these past few days, seemed suddenly to begin flowing again. I hoped that I was not making another mistake. I hoped this was not a dream I was going to wake up from anytime soon.

"Jesse," I said, feeling drunk with happiness, "I don't care about any of that. That kiss . . . that kiss was the best thing that ever happened to me."

I was simply stating a fact. That's all. A fact that I'd been sure he'd already known.

But I guess it came as a surprise to him, since the next thing I knew, he'd pulled me into his arms, and was kissing me all over again.

And it was like the world, which had, for the past few weeks, been off its axis, suddenly righted itself. I was in Jesse's arms, and he was kissing me, and everything was fine. More than fine. Everything was perfect. Because he loved me.

And yeah, okay, maybe that meant he had to move out . . . and yeah, there was the whole Paul thing. I still wasn't too sure what I was going to do about that.

But what did any of that matter? He loved me!

And this time when he kissed me, no one interrupted.

Suze's supernatural misadventures
continue in the sixth Mediator book,

Twilight

The following is an excerpt:

I found the stone exactly where Mrs. Gutierrez had said it would be, beneath the drooping branches of the overgrown hibiscus in her backyard. I shut off the flashlight. Even though there was supposed to have been a full moon that night, by midnight a thick layer of clouds had blown in from the sea, and a dank mist had reduced visibility to nil.

But I didn't need light to see by anymore. I just needed to dig. I sunk my fingers into the wet soft earth and pried the stone from its resting spot. It moved easily and wasn't heavy. Soon I was feeling beneath it for the tin box Mrs. Gutierrez had assured me would be there. . . .

Except that it wasn't. There was nothing beneath my fingers except damp soil.

That's when I heard it—a twig snapping beneath the weight of someone nearby.

I froze. I was trespassing, after all; the last thing I needed was to be dragged home by the Carmel, California, cops.

Again.

Then, with my pulse beating frantically as I tried to figure out how on earth I was going to explain my way out of this one, I recognized the lean shadow—darker than all the others—standing a few feet away. My heart continued to pound in my ears, but now for an entirely different reason.

"You," I said, climbing slowly, shakily, to my feet.

"Hello, Suze." His voice, floating toward me through the mist, was deep, and not at all unsteady . . . unlike my own voice, which had an unnerving tendency to shake when he was around.

It wasn't the only part of me that shook when he was around, either.

But I was determined not to let him know that.

"Give it back," I said, holding out my hand.

He threw back his head and laughed.

"Are you nuts?" he wanted to know.

"I mean it, Paul," I said, my voice steady, but my confidence already beginning to seep away, like sand beneath my feet.

"It's two thousand dollars, Suze," he said, as if I might be unaware of that fact. "Two *thousand*."

"And it belongs to Julio Gutierrez." I sounded sure of myself, even if I wasn't exactly feeling that way. "Not you."

"Oh, right," Paul said, his deep voice dripping with sarcasm. "And what's Gutierrez gonna do, call the cops? He doesn't know it's missing, Suze. He never even knew it was there."

"Because his grandmother died before she had a chance to tell him," I reminded him.

"Then he won't notice, will he?" Despite the darkness, I could tell Paul was smiling. I could hear it in his voice. "You can't miss what you never knew you had."

"Mrs. Gutierrez knows." I'd dropped my hand so he wouldn't see it shaking, but I couldn't disguise the growing unsteadiness in my voice as easily. "If she finds out you stole it, she'll come after you."

"What makes you think she hasn't already?" he asked, so smoothly that the hairs on my arms stood up . . . and not because of the brisk autumn weather, either.

I didn't want to believe him. He had no reason to lie. And obviously, Mrs. Gutierrez had come to him as well as me, anxious for any help she could get. How else could he have known about the money?

Poor Mrs. Gutierrez. She had definitely put her trust the wrong mediator. Because it looked as if Paul hadn't just robbed her. Oh, no. Then, apparently seeing my expression—though I don't know how, since the clouds overhead were thicker than ever—he softened his tone.

"Suze, Suze, Suze," he said, pulling one of his hands from his jacket pocket and moving to drape his arm across my shoulders. "What am I going to do with you?"

I didn't say anything. I don't think I could have spoken if I'd tried. It was hard enough just to breathe. All I could think about was Mrs. Gutierrez, and what he'd done to her. How could someone who smelled so good—the sharp clean scent of his cologne filled my senses—or from whom such warmth radiated—especially welcome, given the chill in the air and the relative thinness of my windbreaker—be so . . .

Well, evil?

"Tell you what," Paul said. I could feel his deep voice reverberating through him as he spoke, he was holding me that close. "I'll split it with you. A grand for each of us."

I had to swallow down something—something

that tasted really bad—before I could reply. "You're sick."

"Don't be that way, Suze," he chided. "You have to admit, it's fair. You can do whatever you want with your half. Mail it back to the Gutierrezes, for all I care. But if you're smart, you'll use it to buy yourself a car now that you finally got your license. You could put a down payment on a decent set of wheels with that kind of change, and not have to worry about sneaking your mom's car out of the driveway after she's fallen asleep—"

"I hate you," I snapped, twisting out from beneath his grip and ignoring the cold air that rushed in to meet the place where his body had been warming mine.

"No, you don't," he said. The moon appeared momentarily from behind the blanket of clouds overhead, just long enough for me to see that his lips were twisted into a lopsided grin. "You're just mad because you know I'm right."

I couldn't believe my ears. Was he serious? "Taking money from a dead woman is the right thing to do?"

"Obviously," he said. The moon had disappeared again, but I could tell from his voice that he was amused. "She doesn't need it anymore.

You and Father Dom. You're a couple of real pushovers, you know. Now I've got a question for you. How'd you know what she was blathering about, anyway? I thought you were taking French, not Spanish."

I didn't answer him right away. That's because I was frantically trying to think of a reply that wouldn't include the word I least liked uttering in his presence, the word that, every time I heard it or even thought it, seemed to cause my heart to do somersaults over in my chest, and my veins to hum pleasantly.

Unfortunately, it was a word that didn't exactly engender the same response in Paul.

Before I could think of a lie, however, he figured it out on his own.

"Oh, right," he said, his voice suddenly toneless. "*Him.* Stupid of me."

Then, before I could think of something to say that would lighten the situation—or at least get his mind off Jesse, the last person in the world I wanted Paul Slater to be thinking about—he said in quite a different tone, "Well, I don't know about you, but I'm beat. I'm gonna call it a night. See you around, Simon."

He turned to go. Just like that, he turned to go.

I knew what I had to do, of course. I wasn't looking forward to it . . . in fact, my heart had pretty much slipped up into my throat, and my palms had gone suddenly, inexplicably damp.

But what choice did I have? I couldn't let him walk away with all that money. I'd tried reasoning with him, and it hadn't worked. Jesse wouldn't like it, but the truth was, there was no other alternative. If Paul wouldn't give up the money voluntarily, well, I was just going to have to take it from him.

I told myself I had a pretty good chance at succeeding, too. Paul had the box tucked into the inside pocket of his jacket. I'd felt it there when he'd put his arm around me. All I had to do was distract him somehow—a good blow to the solar plexus would probably do the job—then grab the box and chuck it through the closest window. The Gutierrezes would freak, of course, at the sound of the breaking glass, but I highly doubted they'd call the cops . . . not when they found two thousand bucks scattered across the floor.

As plans went, it wasn't one of my best, but it was all I had.

I called his name.

He turned. The moon chose that moment to

slip out from behind the thick veil of clouds over-head, and I could see by its pale light that Paul wore an absurdly hopeful expression. The hope-fulness increased as I slowly crossed the grass between us. I suppose he thought for a minute that he'd finally broken me down. Found my weakness. Successfully lured me to the dark side.

And all for the low, low price of a thousand bucks.

Not.

The hopeful look left his face, though, the second he noticed my fist. I even thought that, just for a moment, I caught a look of hurt in his blue eyes, pale as the moonlight around us. Then the moon moved back behind the clouds, and we were once again plunged into darkness.

The next thing I knew, Paul, moving more quickly than I would have thought possible, had seized my wrists in a grip that hurt and kicked my feet out from under me. A second later, I was pinned to the wet grass by the weight of his body and his face just inches from mine.

"That was a mistake," he said, way too casually, considering the force with which I could feel his heart hammering against mine. "I'm rescinding my offer."

His breath, unlike my own, wasn't coming out in ragged gasps, though. Still, I tried to hide my fear from him.

"What offer?" I panted.

"To split the money. I'm keeping it all, now. You really hurt my feelings, you know that, Suze?"

"I'm sure," I said as sarcastically as I could. "Now get off me. These are my favorite low-riders, and you're getting grass stains on them."

But Paul wasn't ready to let me go. He also didn't appear to appreciate my feeble attempt to make a joke out of the situation. His voice, hissing down at me, was deadly serious.

"You want me to make your boyfriend disappear," he asked, "the way I did Mrs. Gutierrez?"

His body was warm against mine, so there was no other explanation for why my heart went suddenly cold as ice, except that his words terrified me to the point that my blood seemed to freeze in my veins.

I couldn't, however, let my fear show. Weakness only seems to trigger cruelty, not compassion, from people like Paul.

"We have an agreement," I said, my tongue and lips forming the words with difficulty because they, like my heart, had gone ice cold with dread.

"I promised I wouldn't kill him," Paul said. "I didn't say anything about keeping him from dying in the first place."

I blinked up at him, uncomprehending.

"What . . . what are you talking about?" I stammered.

"You figure it out," he said. He leaned down and kissed me lightly on my frozen lips. "Good night, Suze."

And then he stood up and vanished into the fog.

It took me a minute to realize I was free. Cool air rushed in to all the places where his body had been touching mine. I finally managed to roll over, feeling as if I'd just suffered a head-on collision with a brick wall. Still, I had enough strength left to call out, "Paul! Wait!"

That's when someone inside the Gutierrez household flicked on the lights. The backyard lit up bright as an airport runway. I heard a window open and someone shout, "Hey, you! What are you doing there?"

I didn't stick around to ask whether or not they planned on calling the cops. I peeled myself up from the ground and ran for the wall I'd scaled a half hour ago. I found my mom's car right where I'd left it. I hopped into it and started my long journey home, cursing a certain fellow mediator—and the grass stains on my new jeans—the whole way.

I had no idea that night how bad things were going to get between Paul and me.

But I was about to find out.

Meg Cabot is also the author of the Princess Diaries series, upon which the Disney movies are based. In the books, though, Princess Mia has yield-sign-shaped hair, lives in New York, and Fat Louie is orange. And those are the least of the differences. The following is a complete list of the Princess Diaries books:

THE PRINCESS DIARIES

THE PRINCESS DIARIES, VOLUME II:
PRINCESS IN THE SPOTLIGHT

THE PRINCESS DIARIES, VOLUME III:
PRINCESS IN LOVE

THE PRINCESS DIARIES, VOLUME IV:
PRINCESS IN WAITING

THE PRINCESS DIARIES, VOLUME IV AND A HALF:
PROJECT PRINCESS

THE PRINCESS DIARIES, VOLUME V:
PRINCESS IN PINK

THE PRINCESS DIARIES, VOLUME VI:
PRINCESS IN TRAINING

THE PRINCESS PRESENT:
A PRINCESS DIARIES BOOK

PRINCESS LESSONS:
A PRINCESS DIARIES BOOK

PERFECT PRINCESS:
A PRINCESS DIARIES BOOK

Aside from the Mediator books
and the Princess Diaries books, Meg
has written several more books:

ALL-AMERICAN GIRL

Samantha Madison saves the president's life . . .
only to have his son fall in love with her. Which
would be fine, except for all the Secret Service
agents following them around.

teen IDOL

Jenny Greenley gives everyone advice, so why
can't she follow her own and find love? Further
complicating matters is the presence of hot
Hollywood star Luke Striker in Jenny's homeroom, of all places.

Nicola and the Viscount

It's 1810, and Nicola Sparks is ready to dive head-
long into her first London Season. Good thing
there's a handsome viscount there to catch her!

Victoria and the Rogue

Lady Victoria Arbuthnot is accustomed to being
right. She isn't always, though, especially when
her own heart is concerned.

But wait!
There's more by Meg:

THE BOY NEXT DOOR

BOY MEETS GIRL

EVERY BOY'S GOT ONE

THE 1-800-WHERE-R-YOU BOOKS:

WHEN LIGHTNING STRIKES

CODE NAME CASSANDRA

SAFE HOUSE

SANCTUARY

For more about Meg and
to read her diary, visit:

www.megcabot.com

Join her online book club at:
www.megcabotbookclub.com